WHISPERS FROM THE DEPTH

THE LAKE MURRAY MURDERS
BOOK 2

STEVEN A JACOBS

OTHER WORKS BY THE AUTHOR

The Disappearance of U-491
Operation Timepiece
The Brazilian Affair
A Call to War
REDEEMED
Wilmington's Lost Fortune
Terror Over the Tarheel State
The Price of Deception
The Silent Witness

Hunter Grey Series
The Whiskey Creek Murders
The Pearson Diaries
Vendetta

Roman Steele Series
The Russian Stratagem
The Hawaiian Connection

Lake Murray Series
The Lake Murray Murders
Whispers From the Depth

WHISPERS FROM THE DEPTH

A Work of Fiction

By: Steven Jacobs

Dedications

To my family and friends who have supported me in putting my stories
down on paper, I thank you from the bottom of my heart.
Also, I want to take the time to thank Gregg Beck, who took the photograph
on which the cover art is based.

"I'm not working on The Great American Novel. All I'm doing, I hope, is
entertaining readers."
Clive Cussler

SPECIAL THANKS

I would like to express my sincere thanks to several businesses that contacted me about being in the book. First, I want to thank the Lake Murray Resort and Marina owners for their help and insight into their property.

Secondly, I want to thank Mr. Wade Campbell of Top Tier Charters of Lake Murray for his help and insight into some of the lake's islands. Lastly, I want to thank Linda Smith of the Palms Grill & Bar in Newberry for reaching out.

I could not include everyone who contacted me in this book, but hopefully, many more books will follow and, with that, more locations.

PROLOGUE

Saluda River Valley 1700s

Gawonii had just finished eating a hearty meal of deer stew, which he had killed earlier in the day. He was sitting by the community fire, talking with his brother Adahy. "I do not like it here, brother. This entire valley has an evil spirit wandering through these woods. I cannot wait to move on from this place."

Adahy picked up a pebble from the ground and tossed it at Gawonii, saying, "Calm yourself, brother; you talk as if you have been in camp with the old women all day long and not out hunting."

As the pebble bounced off his chest, Gawonii replied, "If you are all-knowing, then tell me why we have lost more people since we made camp here. We went for many days without losing a single soul. Even the old and sick ones remained with us, but not anymore. Now, we have lost many since stopping here. I tell you, there is a Uyaga here in this valley."

Adahy laughed aloud at his brother sitting across the fire from him and replied, "There are no evil spirits here! That is old woman talk. Are you sure you don't want to come over and sit beside me so the evil spirit won't get you?"

Before his brother could respond, they heard the voice of Atohi, one of the elders, coming out of the darkness, startling both brothers. "Do not make fun of what you do not understand, Adahy. We Cherokee can feel when something is not right. I have also felt something evil lurking in these woods. There is something not natural here. I have just come from a meeting with the elders, and they feel the same way. There is something not right about this place."

As he gazed into the fire, Atohi said, "You both would do well to get a good night's rest tonight. We are leaving in the morning to go north."

As if on cue, a screaming howl pierced the darkness from close by, startling everyone in camp. Whether young or old, every brave instinctively reached for their weapon to ensure it was within arm's reach.

Atohi saw the braves pulling their weapons closer and smiled. He lowered his voice and said, "You think those will save you from a Uyaga? My father, and his father before him, told us the stories of the Uyaga and how they are not of this world. They are from the spirit world and will come for you in the darkest of nights. All you will see of them are two red eyes glowing like hot coal in the night. They live in your dreams, and that is where they will find you. Put more wood on the fire, for they do not like the light."

Without saying a word, Adahy picked up a piece of wood and tossed it onto the fire to the chuckles of Gawonii because he could tell that Adahy was now spooked after what the elder had said.

Before sunrise the following morning, the women in the camp prepared food for everyone while half of the braves and the elders started packing up the camp. While the food was being prepared and the camp was being packed, the remaining braves kept an ever-vigilant eye on the surrounding trees until sunrise. After the sun rose, the braves that kept guard were pulled back into the camp and began helping pack to speed up the process.

Before long, the fires were extinguished, and the tribe was ready to leave this cursed valley. With village elders in the front setting the pace, women and children in the middle, and braves skirting the edges of the group for protection, the small band of Cherokee made their way out of the valley.

Later that afternoon, and only after the group had left the valley far behind, they stopped for the night. They were exhausted but happy to be away from that valley. That night, the group had a feast, sang songs, and rejoiced late into the night because they were free... free from the Uyaga.

Some two hundred and seventy years later, in the present, a man was camping all alone on a small uninhabited island on Lake Murray known as Goat Island. In the past, before the lake was created, there used to be a homestead on a hill, complete with a small family graveyard.

In 1929, after the dam was completed and the lake began filling in, the area that used to be a homestead became a small island where people came to camp, explore, unwind, and escape the daily struggles of life.

Before the sun went down, the camper lit a fire, making sure to keep it going so that he could cook his dinner. After sitting near the fire, he relaxed in complete silence. Later, the man removed a potato wrapped in aluminum foil from the small cooler and placed it directly into the hot coals, rotating the potato occasionally to ensure it was cooked on all sides.

Once the potato was in the coals and cooking for a few minutes, he pulled a steak from his small cooler and threw some butter and chopped garlic in an iron skillet. Before long, the wonderful smells and sounds of a steak sizzling over an open fire waffled through his campsite.

Smiling at the sights and sounds of his thick T-bone cooking over an open flame, although he was all alone on the island, he said with excitement, "Another four or five minutes on each side, and I will be in heaven."

As if on cue, the man's stomach let out a large rumble. "Settle down, only another few minutes," he told himself.

Before long, the man feasted on his perfectly cooked steak and potato. After eating his meal, he sat back in his folding chair and took in the sounds of the water for a while.

After sitting there for a few minutes, the man thought he heard someone walking in the nearby woods. He pulled the one thousand-lumen flashlight off his hip and shined it into the woods, scanning the area back and forth, and called out, "Is there anyone else here?"

After no one answered, he shrugged, thinking it was not unheard of for more than one group to camp on the island at a time. Still, he walked the island before dark, looking for other campers, and there were none.

Switching the flashlight off and opting to use the much lower-lumen headlamp, the man walked down to the water's edge and gave his pan and utensils a quick rinse.

Returning from the water's edge a few minutes later with a full belly, the man relaxed by the fire for another hour before retiring to his tent for the night. Always prepared, the man took his Sig Saur M17, 9mm, from the small of his back and placed it on the ground beside his sleeping bag should it become necessary. Now, toasty warm and with a full belly, the man slowly drifted off to sleep ... but not for long.

IN THE MIDDLE of the night, the man began to toss and turn, flailing around at an unseen enemy. However, this time, the enemy was in his mind. Ever since returning home from Afghanistan years earlier, the former Marine had been plagued by the same terrible nightmare of the forward observation base he was assigned to coming under intense fire from the Taliban. This resulted in the base being mostly destroyed and many comrades being killed and wounded despite having superior training and firepower.

Usually, while out on the lake, the nightmares don't come, which, truth be known, is why he loved being on the lake. But this time, the nightmares did come, and they came with a vengeance.

Jerking himself awake from the nightmare and drenched in sweat, even though the temperature was in the low fifties, he sat up, taking deep breaths and trying to slow down his heart rate.

When he was doing his deep breathing exercises, he heard it. Freezing momentarily, the man reached for his flashlight and gun ... positive he heard something outside his tent.

Easing out of his sleeping bag, the lone camper quietly pulled the zipper upward, opened the flap of his tent, and shined his flashlight into the darkness. Not seeing anything with his initial sweeps of the flashlight, the camper slid out of his tent to look around.

Standing on the edge of his camp, he saw a dark figure standing there ... watching. "Hey! What are you doing? This is my camp!" The former Marine snapped, "Messing around another man's camp in the dead of night is a good way to get shot."

Oddly enough, the figure initially ignored the man, then bolted into the woods without saying a word. Without thinking of the consequences, the man instinctively gave chase, which was the worst move he could have ever made.

Within moments, the camper and the unknown figure were crashing through the dark woods. Every so often, the camper would get a glimpse of the figure in his flashlight beam, but it would happen so quickly that he couldn't make anything out other than he was dressed in what appeared to be all dark clothes.

The camper managed to keep following the figure for a few minutes before finally losing sight of him near the small graveyard on the island.

After stopping and listening, the camper heard a noise from the graveyard and decided to go in that direction.

As the grave markers came into view, he stopped and listened again, but this time ... nothing. Upset at losing the figure, the camper turned to leave, but he heard something behind him as he turned.

He slowly turned around and saw the figure he had been chasing standing amongst the grave markers. Now annoyed, the camper yelled, "What do you want? Leave me alone!"

In one rapid movement, the camper raised his flashlight to focus on the figure, but at that moment ... the flashlight went out. Now bathed in total darkness, two glowing red eyes pierced the darkness where the figure stood among the grave markers.

Terrified, the camper tried to turn and run, but he was frozen in place as if held there by some unseen force. As hard as he tried, he was unable to move.

The figure slowly approached the camper until they were almost nose to nose. Beyond the red eyes, the camper could see nothing but darkness. Suddenly, a raspy voice said in a low whisper, "I've been waiting for you. I've seen you several times now. You weren't ready then ... but now you are."

Unable to run away, the camper stuttered, "What ... what are you?"

"That does not matter. All that matters is that you follow my instructions. You are to bring me sacrifices ... or I will destroy the dam, killing thousands, and release more ... like me. Bring the sacrifices to me here on these islands ... or many more will die."

The two glowing red eyes slowly backed away from the camper and into the midst of the grave markers. The camper watched in horror as the eyes slowly sank lower and lower until they seemingly melted into the ground and disappeared.

The next thing he knew, the camper was waking up in his tent the following morning. He sat up confused and thought to himself, *was that real, or was it a new nightmare?*

Less than an hour later, the man packed up his camp and was loading his boat when he saw them. As he was wading out to his boat just offshore, he glanced down and saw what appeared to be the same two glowing red eyes underneath the water. As soon as he saw the eyes, he heard, or instead felt, a voice inside his mind saying, "Remember what I said ... I'll be waiting."

1

Jeramy Donahue pulled up to the quaint little Airbnb after his drive down from Charlotte. He had come to Lake Murray several years ago while recovering from a string of stress-induced panic attacks stemming from his job.

After becoming an investment banker five years ago, everything else in his life stopped. In the years after he got his dream job, his fiancé left him, he started drinking heavily, friends distanced themselves from him ... and then the panic attacks began.

Doctors had told him if he didn't slow down and start taking breaks, he would end up having a heart attack. Since then, he decided to slow down, focus on his health, and mend relationships with friends and family. One of the main things he started doing was going to the Lake Murray Resort and Marina every eight months to a year for solo weekend getaways.

After parking, Jeramy got out and stretched for the first time since he left Charlotte over an hour and a half beforehand. He then took a deep breath of fresh, clean country air. Once he grabbed his belongings from the back of his BMW 4 Series Coupe, he walked up the steps, entered the code into the door lock, and strolled right in.

Even though he was alone, he exclaimed, "Free at last!"

He plopped down on the couch for a few minutes, where he saw a stack of books on a little table in the corner beside the sofa. Picking the top book off of the stack, he read aloud, "*The Lake Murray Murders by Steven Jacobs*. That looks interesting. I may start reading that after getting something to eat and securing a boat for the weekend."

After settling in, Jeramy walked across to the main building, The Cove, for a bite to eat and to see if the bar was open yet. As soon as he walked in, Jeramy almost literally bumped into Laurie, whom he recognized from previous visits. Laurie said, "Hi! Matt and I are glad to see you back. How's it going?"

"It's going good so far. I just got here a little while ago. I was coming over to get a bite to eat, then hit the bar," Jeramy said with a smile.

Before she walked off, Laurie asked, "Is there anything I can do for ya while I'm here?"

"Actually, there is. I want to go out fishing tomorrow. Do you know if you have any boats available?"

"I'm pretty sure we do. I think some pontoon boats are in use, but I think I can get you into the center console boat tomorrow if you want."

"That would be perfect," Jeramy replied, trying not to get his hopes up.

"Why don't you grab a table in the restaurant, and I'll come find you when I know something?" Laurie said.

"Sounds good," Jeramy said as he walked into the restaurant.

Once seated, Jeramy looked over the menu and decided on the Bourbon Burger and fries. While waiting for his burger and fries, Jeramy looked over the fishing reports from the lake on his phone.

As he reviewed the fishing reports, Laurie walked up smiling and said, "You're all set for tomorrow. I have reserved a center console for you. The weather's looking good, so you should have fun."

Jeramy smiled brightly and said, "Thank you so much!"

About that time, the waitress returned with his order, and Laurie took this as her cue to leave, allowing Jeramy to eat his huge burger in peace. After Jeramy ate his burger, he walked out back and onto a massive deck where he viewed the sunset in peace and quiet.

After the sun went down, he walked a short distance over to the bar, where he listened to a local singer and drank several shots of high-end Vodka.

Later in the night, after dropping quite a bit of money at the bar and having quite the buzz, Jeramy walked back to the Airbnb he had rented for a good night's sleep.

WAKING EARLY THE FOLLOWING MORNING, Jeramy got dressed, took headache medicine for his hangover, and walked to the marina, where Laurie had procured the boat that was waiting for him.

The further Jeramy walked onto the dock, the more excited he became. Before moving to Charlotte, he grew up near the ocean and missed cruising the waters of the intercoastal waterways. He said good morning to several other early-morning fishermen as he walked down the dock and began to load his gear onto the boat. As he untied the boat and pushed off from the dock, Jeramy thought, *One day, I'm going to either move here or back home.*

With the ease of a seasoned professional, Jeramy put the boat in reverse and slowly backed away from the dock before spinning the boat around and slowly motoring out into the cove. Once in deeper water, he could speed up and let loose for the trip to his favorite fishing spot on the lake. Nobody knew it then, but those fellow anglers who would see Jeramy Donahue loading his boat and pushing away from the dock would be some of the last people ever to see him alive.

Later that day, it was reported over the news that a boat had been found floating in the lake with no one aboard. It was not long before a Saluda County sheriff's deputy pulled into the parking lot of the Lake Murray Resort with a warrant in hand, should it become necessary. Onlookers watched intently as the deputy walked inside and asked to speak to someone in charge.

Before long, Laurie and her husband, Matt, met with the deputy who told them that one of their boats had been found floating in the lake with no one aboard. Immediately, Laurie knew who had now been declared missing—Jeramy Donahue.

After talking with the deputy briefly, Matt and Laurie escorted the deputy to the Airbnb Donahue rented for the weekend. After telling them to stand outside on the grass, the deputy went inside and found nothing amiss.

Detectives showed up to investigate and interview people, but the main search was out on the lake, where it appeared that Jeramy might have fallen overboard.

The Saluda County Sheriff's Department, the South Carolina Division of Natural Resources, and the Lexington County Sheriff's Department dive team searched multiple areas. Eventually, the search for either Jeramy Donahue or his remains was called off days later after nothing was found.

2

Three weeks later, the Simpson family boat nudged up to the edge of Goat Island for their annual spring camping trip. The family had camped on several of the islands in the past, but for some reason, the Goat Island camping trip had always been their 'kickoff' to the summer months on the lake, and this spring, it was no different.

While the kids jumped into the water's edge from the boat and waded ashore, Kyle and his wife, Susie, secured the boat and began hauling things to the shoreline from where the boat was anchored just offshore.

The Simpson's two children, Jayden, age 13, and Sofia, age 10, stayed near the shoreline for a few minutes before slowly wandering into the nearby woods.

"Come on back, guys!" Kyle shouted, "You know how this works. Your mom and I bring the stuff to shore, and you stay in sight until we get everything ashore and the camp is set up. That way, we can all go exploring."

"Yeah!" Both kids squealed with excitement.

It wasn't long before all the supplies were transferred from the boat to the island, and about thirty minutes later, the family had their campsite picked out and the tent set up, ready for a fun weekend.

After everything in camp was set up, the family of four grabbed their backpacks and set out for a short hike around the island, stopping at the small graveyard on the island.

The family had been hiking for about twenty minutes or so, just relaxing, taking in the scenery, and having a good family outing; however, that was about to change in a matter of minutes.

While Kyle and Susie leisurely strolled through the trees, they stopped at the small graveyard, as they always do, to pay homage to those who had come before them. While reading the grave markers for the first time this year, both noticed the kids had wandered off a little too far.

Kyle called out, "Jaden ... Sophia, come back. We can't see you!"

Both Kyle and Susie suddenly heard Sophia's scream from the nearby woods. Instantly, both parents bolted from the grave markers and into the woods from where Sophia's scream came from.

Kyle shouted, "SOPHIA! JAYDEN! ANSWER ME!" as he crashed through the woods and underbrush with his wife on his heels.

Moments later, Kyle plowed through a small section of thick underbrush and saw both of their kids running in their direction. Kyle and Susie grabbed their children and hugged them tightly for a moment before asking, "What happened? Why did you scream?"

Sniffling and with tears running down her face, Sophia said, "There's another grave back there that wasn't there before."

"What do you mean another grave?" Susie asked as she looked at Kyle, "We've been all over this island, and there are no more graves anywhere else but back there."

"There is another grave over there, but we can see the bones and stuff. It's gross, and it stinks!" Jayden replied.

Kyle and Susie stared at each other momentarily as they both realized something was terribly wrong. Kyle said, "I'm sure it's just an animal or something. Sometimes deer are found out here."

"No! It's not a deer. It's a person," Sophia said, adamantly.

Susie looked at Kyle and said, "Go look, please. I'll stay here with the kids."

"You guys, stay here and don't move. I'm going to have a look. Relax, I'm sure it's nothing," Kyle said.

Kyle slowly walked in the direction his kids had come from, and before long, he got a whiff of a rancid and rotten smell. Being ever so careful, Kyle kept going until he could see something on the ground not far away.

Finally, when he was still about ten yards away, he did not want to go closer due to the smell, but it was close enough. There was absolutely no doubt that it was what remained of a body—and it was definitely human.

Kyle backed away from the area and returned to where Susie and the kids were a short distance away. Before he even said anything, Susie could tell by the look on his face that something was terribly wrong. "Let's ... let's, uh, go back to the campsite," Kyle said, trying not to worry the kids.

"Well, what was it, Dad? Was it a dead body?" Jayden asked.

Before Kyle could say anything, Jayden's sister Sophia started crying and said, "I'm scared! I wanna go home!"

"Well, we can't go home right now, sweetie." Susie said as she knelt down to comfort her daughter, "It's going to be ok. I promise."

A few minutes later, the family reached their campsite, and once they were near their boat, Kyle walked a short distance away and called 911 to report the body they had just found.

After the 911 call was placed, a patrol boat from the South Carolina Department of Natural Resources arrived not long afterward.

Susie and the kids waited at the campsite while Kyle stood at the water's edge and helped the game warden secure his boat. Thankful to have some type of professional help there, Kyle already felt better.

"I'm Game Warden Russell Watts with SCDNR. Are you the campers who reported the body on the island?"

Breathing a sigh of relief, Kyle replied, "We sure are, and we're glad you're here!"

Kyle stepped back as Watts lept the short distance from the SCDNR's bow onto dry land. Kyle and Watts shook hands for the first time. Watts asked, "So, tell me what happened."

As the two walked the short distance to the family's camp, Kyle replied, "We've only been here an hour or so. We made camp, and the kids were excited to explore the island since it was our first time out this season. After setting up camp, we went for a hike. We went to the grave markers as we usually do, and then the kids went a little bit ahead of us, and that's when they found the body."

As they walked into the camp, Kyle introduced the game warden to the kids, who asked, "Are we in trouble?"

"Oh, no, you're not in any trouble at all," Watts said as he squatted down to face Sophia. But I do need to ask you a question, though. Did either of you touch anything?"

About that time, Jayden made a face and said, "Ewww, no! It was gross and stinky."

Watts smiled and said, "Okay, then. How about you guys stay here with your mom while your dad and I look at what you found?"

"Ok," Sophia and Jayden replied. Watts stood up, looked at Kyle, and said, "Show me."

Kyle looked at Susie and said, "Keep an eye on the kids. We will be back soon."

Watts waited for the pair to get a short distance from the family when he asked, "Did you see what the kids were talking about?"

"Yeah, as soon as we made sure they were ok, I went to have a look for myself."

"And since you called 911, I assume it is a body, correct?" Watts asked.

"Yeah, it's a person, but it's more than that."

"What do you mean?" Watts asked.

"You just gotta see for yourself. It looks … strange."

As they walked past the grave markers known to be on the island, Kyle replied, "The body looks almost … posed or something. I could be wrong. I didn't get too close so I wouldn't disturb anything."

A few moments later, Kyle stopped and said, "Okay, we're getting close. It should be straight ahead about ten more yards or so. I'm gonna stay here if that's ok with you. I don't care to see ... or smell it again."

"Not a problem," Watts said as he left Kyle and slowly walked in the direction Kyle had pointed.

Watts had scarcely walked twenty feet when he started smelling the rotting smell of decay. Pressing forward, the scent became increasingly overpowering, but in the leaves just ahead, he could make out a body's remains.

Watts stopped briefly, took a rag from a cargo pocket on his pants, folded it several times, and put it over his nose to staunch the smell. When he was ready, he moved cautiously closer until he was within a few feet of the remains. As he examined the area, he could immediately tell there was no doubt it was a human body, and the camper had been right; the body had been most definitely posed.

After examining the remains for a moment, he cautiously backed up and returned to where Kyle was watching, "Well?"

"You would be correct," Watts said. That is a body, and I believe you are also correct about it being posed."

As they returned to the family's campsite, Kyle asked, "So, now what?"

"Well, I will need to make a couple of phone calls, but you guys will have to stay in camp for a while. Needless to say, your camping trip will probably end early."

"It's ok. The kids want to go home now anyway."

"I don't doubt that," Watts replied, "but I need you guys to hang around a little longer. A sheriff's deputy will want to talk to you before you leave the island. You can go ahead and start packing up, though, because I'm sure once the deputy gets here, they're going to close off the island." Watts pointed in the direction of his boat and said, "I'm going to go right over there for a moment. I have to call this in."

Watts walked a short distance away out of earshot and began notifying his chain of command and the Lexington County Sheriff's Department. Within twenty minutes, a boat from the Lexington

County Sheriff's Marine Unit was coming into view around the island's tip.

The Simpson family watched as the sheriff's boat slowly pulled up to the island near the SCDNR boat. A few minutes later, the game warden returned to the camp with another man who identified himself as Officer Brett Gibson from the Lexington County Sheriff's Marine Unit. Once again, Kyle and his wife Susie told the officer what happened. After listening to what they had to say, Watts took Officer Gibson to where the body was found.

As soon as Gibson got within five yards of where the body was situated, he said, "I've seen enough. I'm gonna call dispatch and get the ball rolling. Where is the nearest boat landing?"

After thinking a moment, Watts replied, "That would probably be the boat ramp at Bush River Road and Highway Six by the dam."

Gibson replied, "Perfect. I will call it in and have detectives and the crime scene guys stage there. Can you get them here? I can help once the first boat group gets here, but I can't leave the crime scene unattended now."

Watts replied, "Sure, that's not a problem."

DETECTIVE AMY STONE had finished her first cup of coffee and was already halfway through her second cup while working on paperwork from her previous case when Lexington County Sheriff's Chief of Detectives Stephen Boone walked up to Stone's desk and said, "I need to see you in my office."

Stone looked up and said, "What's going on Chief?"

"Your new partner is here, that's all," Boone replied.

"I didn't think I would, but I'm actually starting to like working alone," Stone replied flatly.

"Too bad. You knew it was only going to be for a short time. Besides, you're going to like this guy," Boone said with a smile.

"Really, now," Stone said, perking up. "Is he handsome?"

"Not my department," Boone said. "He's in my office now. Come on, I'll introduce you to him."

Stone hopped up and followed Boone back to his office, where she laid eyes on her new partner for the first time.

When Boone and Stone walked in, she saw a massive mountain of a man sitting in one of the chairs across from Boone's desk. Boone said, "Raylon Cross, I want you to meet your new partner, Amy Stone."

As soon as Boone began introducing Cross, he stood and extended his huge hand out to Stone to shake hands with her.

"Good morning. It's a pleasure," Cross said with a huge smile and a deep Southern accent. "I've heard great things about you."

Stone was momentarily stunned at the size of her new partner. He had to be at least six feet, four inches tall, and probably weighed three hundred pounds. Everything from his huge thighs to his massive chest and arms said Raylon Cross was a formidable man indeed.

His dark, ebony skin and massive size were offset by a warm and friendly, somewhat round face that showed a perfect set of white teeth when he smiled.

"Uh, hi. Nice to meet you," Stone said with a smile, "Geeze, did you have to turn sideways to get in the boss' office? How big are you?"

Smiling at Stone, Cross said, "Six, four and about two ninety-five or so, depending on the time of day. I was a competitive weightlifter for a while. People who know me call me "Big Nims," the beast of a man said warmly.

"Big Nims? Why's that?" Stone asked.

Smiling, he said, "Back home in Alabama, my mother is a history teacher. Well, one day, when I was young, she was researching World War I for a lesson plan that she had coming up, and she saw a photo of a man with very similar facial features as I have. She printed the photograph and kept it on her desk. Whenever I looked at it, she told me to always smile. Even in the rough times ... smile."

Cross took his phone out and showed Stone and Boone a black-and-white photo on his phone of a black man in a World War I US military uniform holding a gas mask, smiling from ear to ear, and showing off a perfect set of white teeth who had strikingly similar features to Cross.

Both Boone and Stone were shocked at how much the two looked alike. "Damn. What happened to the man in the photograph?" Boone asked from the other side of his desk.

"Nobody knows what happened to him. The original picture in the National Museum of African American History and Culture lists his name only as Big Nims of the 366th Infantry and gives a date of 1918. Besides that, there is no record of his real name or if he survived the war. I'd like to think he survived and had a long life, but nobody knows what happened to him."

"It's crazy how much you two look alike," Stone said, "not to mention that this picture was taken over a hundred years ago."

"Yeah, I'd like to think that somehow we're related," Cross said with a warm smile.

About that time, the phone on Boone's desk rang. Picking it up, he said, "Boone here." Both Stone and Cross were quiet for a few minutes while Boone was on the phone, then Boone said, "Okay, I got it," as he scribbled something down on a piece of paper on his desk. He hung up the phone and said, "Well, Cross, I wanted to break you in a little slower, but it seems like you'll have to hit the ground running. We just got a call about a body being dumped. Are you up for it?"

"Not a problem," Cross said, "Where are we going?"

"The boat ramp at Bush River Road and Number Six," Boone replied.

"That's not exactly a quiet spot for something to go down," Stone replied.

"Well, there's one hitch. You guys are meeting an SCDNR boat there, and he's gonna take you to the crime scene. I want you two to go have a look before we start moving people out there."

"Boat?" Cross asked with raised eyebrows.

"Where exactly is this body?" Stone asked.

"That's the thing, a family found a body while camping on Goat Island."

"So, we have to take a boat to get to the crime scene?" Cross asked.

"Yeah, is there a problem?" Boone asked.

Hesitating for a split second, Cross said, "No ... no problem, it's just that it's true about what they say. My people and water don't exactly mix."

Stone replied with a sideways grin, "Don't worry, big man. If something happens, I'll save you."

Cross laughed, looked at Stone, and said, "Oh, I see, it's like that. How are you gonna bust me out in front of the boss on my first day?"

Boone laughed, saying, "Shots fired within five minutes of you two being partnered up. This is going to be great! I can see this coming."

3

S tone and Cross hopped up and started towards Stone's car. "Do you know where this boat ramp is?" Cross asked.

"Yep, sure do," Stone replied. "My last partner and I started his last case there."

As they got into Stone's unmarked cruiser, Cross asked, "Since we're on the subject of your last partner, mind if I ask what happened to him?"

While Stone pulled out of the parking spot and onto the main road, she paused momentarily and replied, "Nothing bad. He had been on the job for twenty-plus years. At the end of our last case, he retired."

"I see," the big man replied. "How long will it take us to get there?"

"To the boat ramp? Not long, maybe fifteen minutes," Stone replied, "Why?"

"No reason. Just wondering, trying to get my bearings. I'm still getting used to the layout of the area. That's all," Cross replied.

"What brought you here to Lexington?" Stone asked.

"Back home in Alabama, I was from a small police force, and once I set my sights on my detective's badge, I figured I would have to move. I wanted to go to a place where it was bigger but still had that hometown feel. So, how big is this lake exactly?"

Stone replied, "It's somewhere in the neighborhood of forty miles long and fourteen miles wide and about two hundred feet deep at the deepest part. I'm not sure exactly; there are nearly a dozen named islands and quite a few that aren't named."

Cross' eyes widened, and he said, "Man! That's one huge lake."

"Yes, it is," Stone replied, smiling with pride. You'll find that we South Carolinians love our lake. People come from all over the United States to go fishing or take vacations here. So, when something happens on the lake, we take notice."

Stone and Cross continued chatting on the way to the boat ramp and simply getting to know one another. I don't see a wedding ring, so I'm guessing you're not married," Stone said.

"No, not married, no kids or anything. I had a girlfriend some time ago, but she broke up with me about six months ago because of the job, and I just haven't felt like getting back out there again. Not yet, anyway. What about you?" Cross asked.

Stone smiled and said, "Definitely not married, no kids, and as of a few months ago, no boyfriend either. His job and mine didn't work too well. He is an FBI agent I met while working on a case. We hit it off great for a while, but it flamed out quickly once he had to go back to Washington."

"Sorry to hear that," Cross said.

Before long, Stone said, "You ready to see the lake?"

"I guess so," Cross said.

"Good, because we will be crossing the dam here in just a few minutes," Stone replied.

Stone grinned at Cross' reaction as the lake came into view. "Man! You weren't kidding about the size of the lake!" Cross replied with his Alabama twang. "And we gotta go out there?"

"Yep, sure do," Stone smirked.

"It's a nice and bright day, so the LMM won't be out."

"I really don't want to know, but what's the LMM?"

"Lake Murray monster," Stone replied. "Some say there's something living in the lake that's not supposed to be there, but I don't believe it."

"Wait a minute," Cross said wild-eyed, "ain't nobody said nothing about no damned monster! What in the hell is this thing supposed to be?"

"Nobody knows; rumor has it it's like our very own Loch Ness Monster."

Cross began furiously shaking his head from side to side, saying, "Nope, nope, nope! Hell naw! I'll stay here with the car, you can go and take pictures, but I ain't goin'!"

Stone couldn't hold it in any longer and burst out laughing, saying, "Just playing with ya, big man! There's nothing out there that's going to get you, I promise."

Cross breathed a sigh of relief and said, "I can see it already. You're going to be a pain in my ass. Aren't you?"

Stone giggled and said, "Now you know the real reason my last partner retired," as she pulled into a parking spot.

The pair got out and slowly made their way down to the dock near the boat ramp, where there was a boat from the South Carolina Department of Natural Resources tied up and waiting for them.

As they walked out to the end of the dock where the SCDNR boat was tied up, Stone said, "I think you're waiting for us. I'm Detective Amy Stone, and this is my partner, Detective Raylon Cross."

The man wearing a green uniform and baseball hat adjusted his gun belt and said, "Yep, I'm your ride. I'm Officer Watts with SCDNR."

Cross looked at Stone and quietly asked, "What's SCDNR?"

Stone replied, "It's the South Carolina Department of Natural Resources. They are the guys who enforce laws for the state for hunting, fishing, poaching ... things like that."

"So, they're game wardens?" Cross asked.

"The one and the same," Stone replied.

"You could have just led with that," Cross replied, smiling.

Watts looked Cross up and down and said, "You have to sit in the middle, for sure, as he pointed him to the bench-style seat in front of the boat's center console."

"No problem, but why?" Cross asked.

"Because of your big size, staying closer to the boat's centerline will help the ride be ... smoother," Watts replied.

"What about me? Where do you want me to sit?" Stone asked.

Watts smiled and said, "I have a special place for you ... right here beside me."

Stone smiled coyly as she brushed a strand of hair behind her ear and said, "No problem."

Watts opened a built-in storage compartment and handed Stone and Cross a life vest, saying, "Here, put these on. I haven't lost anybody yet, and I don't intend on losing anyone today."

"How in the hell does this thing work?" Cross asked as he struggled to put his life vest on.

"Big man, you gotta open your straps all the way and then just slide into it, just like a bulletproof vest," Watts replied.

While Cross struggled to get into his vest, Watts looked at Stone and said, "Here, let me help you." He helped Stone into her vest and cinched it down like it was supposed to be.

After taking a few minutes to help Stone and Cross put on their life vests, Watts untied his boat from the dock and slowly backed away. Once clear from the dock, Watts turned the boat around and said, "Hang on," before pushing the throttle lever forward. Before long, they were moving at a fast pace across Lake Murray heading towards Goat Island.

AFTER THE SHORT run to Goat Island, Watts slowed the boat and circled the island until they spotted the Lexington County Sheriff's patrol boat tied up beside another private boat. Watts expertly pulled in beside the two boats, tied off, and cut his engine.

It took another few minutes to get ashore, but finally, Stone looked at Cross and asked, "So, how was the ride?"

Cross smiled and said, "I gotta admit, it wasn't half bad."

"That's good," Stone said while they waited for Watts to get ashore.

After securing the boat and joining Stone and Cross on shore, Watts took the two detectives to the campsite where the family who had found the body was sitting along with Officer Brett Gibson from the Lexington County Sheriff's Marine Unit.

Gibson shook hands with the two detectives and then introduced them to the Simpson family, who had found the body. Once the family told their story again, Stone got their contact information and said it was okay for them to leave.

After interviewing the family, Stone and Cross had Officer Gibson take them to where the body was located while Watts helped the family finish breaking down their camp and get everything to their boat.

After a short walk, Gibson said, "It's just up ahead about ten more yards or so. Do either of you have anything to cover your noses?"

"Is it that bad?" Cross asked.

"Well, I'm no expert by any means, but I'd say the body has been here a while." Gibson replied, "So yeah, it's pretty bad."

Stone looked at Cross and said, "I can manage. How about you?"

"Don't worry about me," Cross said. "Let's see what we have."

"Uh, if it's all the same to you guys, I've seen it. I don't need to see it again ... or smell it," Gibson replied.

Stone smiled and said, "No problem. Just hang out here for a few minutes."

Cross and Stone walked a few more yards, and that is when they saw and began to smell the body. The pair walked as close as they dared to get without contaminating the area where the body was dumped.

What they saw before them, covered partially with leaves, were the remains of what appeared to be a man lying on his back. His legs had been placed together, and his arms were folded onto his chest. His hands were folded over one another, not unlike mummies of ancient Egypt.

"Damn," Stone said, "Look at how his hands have been folded across his chest."

"Yeah, I see that," Cross replied, "and look at how straight his legs are. There's no doubt this body has been posed. This is not your normal body dump."

"Nope, not at all," Stone replied. "Not only that, there was no attempt to hide the body. It looks as if the body was simply laid out on the ground. If someone took the time to bring the body all the way out here, they would have had ample time to bury it. If they had done so, chances are it would have been years before the body was found, if ever."

Cross replied, "I know this place is remote, but maybe the killer was interrupted or simply thought the body would not be discovered here?"

"I kind of doubt it," Stone replied. The islands on the lake are a popular spot for camping. It would only be a matter of time before someone found the body. Whoever dumped this body either wanted or needed it to be found."

Stone took out her phone to see if she had cell service, which she did, so she called Chief Boone, making sure to put the call on speaker so Cross could hear the conversation.

After a few rings, Stone heard, "Boone here."

"Hey, Chief, it's me, Stone. There's no doubt ... we have a body. We're going to need forensics and the whole kit and caboodle. There's more, though. This body was not just dumped. It was staged."

After pausing a moment, Boone replied, "Ok, I will get the ball rolling. I will call SCDNR and see if I can get another boat to make transferring people to and from the island easier. You guys just sit tight. It's going to be a while."

"Wonderful," Stone replied.

Once Stone had finished talking to Boone, she and Cross backed up a short distance from the body to preserve the scene. " Okay, so now what do we do?" Cross asked.

"Well, for one, we wait. And we can get to know each other better while we wait."

"Yeah, kinda like Watts wanted to get to know you better on the way over to the island," Cross replied.

"What are you talking about?" Stone asked. "He was just being nice."

"Yeah, sure he was," Cross shot back. "The only time that dude took his eyes off you was when he was driving the boat to get us over here."

"Aww, that's sweet," Stone said as she patted him on his beefy shoulder. "We just met a little while ago, and my new partner is getting jealous already."

"Am not," Cross replied with a huff.

"It's okay, big man. He didn't mean anything by it," Stone said with a giggle. Come on, let's help get this family off the island."

BEFORE THE FAMILY LEFT, Stone talked to them again, ensuring they knew it was an active crime scene investigation and that they should not speak to anyone about it. Mr. and Mrs. Simpson assured the detective they would not say anything and would do their best to keep the kids quiet as well.

Fifteen minutes after the family that called in the body left the island, one of Watts' counterparts arrived on another SCDNR boat, and the process of ferrying coroners and crime scene technicians to and from the boat landing began.

The first set of new officers to see the body were crime scene technicians who specialized in photographing, making sketches, and collecting evidence from the area. Cross escorted them to the body and pointed out a few things for them to ensure that they were photographed, including the victim's hands and the way they were posed.

While the technicians began their work, Watts took his boat and returned to the boat landing to retrieve another group of crime scene technicians, including the interim coroner, Sandeep Singh.

Stone and Cross watched as the crime scene technicians and

photographers did their work until they heard a boat approaching the island. Once they heard the motor's pitch slow, they knew a new group of technicians was about to arrive. Stone and Cross returned to the impromptu staging area for the crime scene investigators and observed as the next boat arrived.

As Watts pulled the boat back up to the island, Cross leaned in and whispered to Stone, "Who's that with the turban on?"

"That is none other than our interim coroner, Dr. Sandeep Singh. Don't let him hear you call his headwear a turban. He will quickly correct you and tell you it's a traditional Sikh Pagri."

"Okay then," Cross replied.

Sensing Cross's uneasiness, Stone smiled and said, "He's a very nice guy. Don't worry."

Once Dr. Singh and his assistants were on the island with their body bag and gear, Stone and Cross walked over and said, "Hello, doctor. I want you to meet my new partner, Detective Raylon Cross."

Cross and Singh shook hands, and with a slight nod of his head, Dr. Singh said, "It's a pleasure to meet you, Detective Cross. Now, would you two mind showing us where the body is located so we may get to work?"

"Right this way, doctor," Cross replied as he and Stone led Singh and his assistants to the body's location. Before beginning their work, Singh talked to the crime scene technicians to ensure everything had been documented before they started the arduous task of examining the body.

Within thirty minutes of arriving, Singh walked over to where Cross and Stone were standing to update them. "I'd say your victim was dumped out here ... perhaps three weeks to a month ago. There are no obvious signs of trauma that I can see out here. I won't know any more until I get the body back for a complete post-mortem examination."

Singh continued, as if asking a question, saying, "If everything has been photographed and the forensic techs are ready, I will move the body so they can take more photographs and look for any additional evidence. I'll collect the body and get it ready for transport so the crime scene techs can finish their work."

Stone replied, "Yeah, sure, doctor, the forensic techs want to bag the hands before you collect the body and get it ready. When will you know something?"

"It's tough to say. The body is in pretty rough shape at this point."

Cross asked, "Other than it being a white male, what else can you tell at this point?"

Singh thought momentarily and said, "Well, as you said, the body is that of a white male, approximately six feet tall, with brown hair. There are no visible tattoos or scars. Getting fingerprints will be a bit of a challenge. Our best shot at finding out exactly who this person is will be either with DNA or dental records."

"Okay, doctor. Thank you. Yeah, go ahead and get this poor soul out of here so we can hopefully notify next of kin to give him a decent burial," Stone said matter of factly.

Cross and Stone stayed on Goat Island for another hour with other crime scene technicians and photographers while a grid search was conducted of the area, using the spot where the body was located as the center of the grid. After nothing else was found, the island was turned back over to SCDNR, which reopened it to boaters and campers.

Once they were ready to leave, SCDNR Officer Watts made sure he was the warden who took the two detectives back to the mainland. Once again, Cross was left to fend for himself while Watts helped Stone into her life vest and put her beside him for the ride back.

Of the several boats that SCDNR had to keep at bay during the investigation on the island, one hung around all day, not fishing or sightseeing ... just watching. As the boat carrying the two detectives returned to the dock, the individual in the boat followed, taking photos as he went.

Before long, Watts was rocketing back across the lake toward the boat landing where he had met the two earlier in the morning. As the boat landing came into sight, Watts backed off the throttle, which, in turn, slowed the boat until they were easing up to a nearby dock.

Both detectives stayed seated until Watts tied the boat up to the dock and shut the motor off. After that, Watts helped Stone slip out of her life vest and step over to the dock. After Cross got his vest off and stepped onto the pier, she asked, "Are you hungry?"

Before Cross could answer, Watts butted into the conversation and said, "I can't leave my boat. I'm on duty."

Cross stared at Watts before responding to Stone, "I could eat."

Watts held his hands up and said, "Sorry, I hoped—uh, thought she was talking to me." Watts couldn't resist taking a parting shot at Cross, winked at Stone, and said, "Call me if you need to return to the crime scene. The sunsets on the lake are beautiful."

Cross turned to face Watts, who wisely hopped back into his boat, saying, "Well, I guess I've worn out my welcome. I'll be off now."

As Stone and Cross watched Watts untie from the dock and slowly back away, Watts put his thumb and little finger up to the side of his head and mouthed the words *call me* to Stone before turning around and motoring out of the marina.

4

"So, since that unpleasantness is over with, what did you have in mind to eat?" Cross asked.

"That kind of depends on you," Stone replied.

"What do you mean?"

"There's a place we eat quite often that's not far from the office and has good food. The only thing is ... there's not much there that's good for you."

"Sounds like my kind of place," Cross replied. "Lead on."

Before long, the pair pulled into the Old Mill in the heart of Lexington. After getting out of the car and walking up the sidewalk, Cross saw the sign over the door and said aloud, "Creekside Restaurant, it sounds like a good spot."

"It is," Stone replied. "A lot of us from the department often come here to eat."

As soon as they walked in, the pair heard the all-too-familiar "Hey y'all!" from one of the waitresses. "Just you two today?"

"Yep, just us," Stone replied with a smile.

"I don't have anything open right now unless you want to sit at the bar," the waitress suggested.

Stone glanced at Cross, who shook his head in agreeance, saying, "That's fine with me if it's okay with you."

"We'll take it," Stone said with a smile.

A few moments later, Stone and Cross were seated on barstools in front of the large television hanging over the massive pass-through, which allowed customers to watch their orders being made.

One man in the kitchen glanced over his shoulder and saw Detective Stone sitting there, then smiled and waved at her.

Stone smiled and waved back, and after the man finished what he was doing, he walked out of the kitchen behind the bar to where Stone and Cross were seated.

Before Stone could say anything, the man said, "Did the old man finally give it up?"

Giggling, Stone replied, "Yeah, Clayton finally retired. After that last case, he decided to hang it up. Anyway, I'd like to introduce you to my new partner, Raylon Cross." Stone looked at Cross and said, "This is Kirt, the owner."

Kirt wiped his hands off quickly on the apron he was wearing and reached across the counter to shake hands with Stone's new partner. Cross shook hands with Kirt, saying, "Nice to meet you."

Stone watched Kirt shake hands with Cross and, for the first time, saw his watch peeking out from under his tailored button-up shirt.

"Well, I hate to do it, but I gotta get back in the kitchen and get these orders out."

"Sure, no problem. Do your thing," Cross said with a smile.

As soon as Kirt walked off, the waitress took his place and asked, "What would you two like to drink?"

"Water's fine with me," Cross replied.

"And I know what you want. You're getting sweet tea, aren't you?" The waitress said to Stone.

"Yep, sure am," Stone replied.

"Whatcha want to eat?" The waitress asked.

"What's good?" Cross asked.

Before Stone could say anything, the waitress smiled and said, "It's all good. It just depends on you."

Stone said, "I agree, but their cheeseburgers and fries are fantastic."

"Sounds like a winner," Cross replied.

"Make that two of them," Stone replied.

After the waitress walked off, Stone asked, "Can I see your watch?"

"Why?" Cross asked hesitantly.

"Come on, hand it over. I know a Rolex when I see one."

Cross reluctantly slipped the watch off his wrist and handed it to Stone for her to admire. Letting out a whistle as she admired the watch's color. It started with blue at the twelve o'clock position and faded into black the closer it reached the six o'clock position on the bezel. Stone replied in a low voice, "That's the Rolex Deepsea. That's a fourteen-thousand-dollar watch." Stone smiled and said, "And how did we come by this on a sheriff's salary, hmmm?"

Stone returned the watch to Cross, who put it back on his wrist, smiled, and said, "Remember in the Chief's office when I told you I used to be a competitive bodybuilder?"

"Yeah, I remember." Stone said.

"Well, I was good. Like, really good, and actually won a few tournaments. This watch was the trophy for second place in one of my competitions."

"Damn, that was second?" Stone said wild-eyed. "If that was second, what in the hell was the first prize?"

Cross shrugged and said, "I don't remember. A lot has happened since I won that in 2014."

"Wow! 2014," Stone repeated. "I was just coming on the job about that time."

"Why did you become a cop?" Cross asked.

Stone shrugged her shoulders and said, "Eh, it's a long story, and you don't want to hear me telling you about my whole life story on your first day."

"Sure I do."

At about that time, the waitress returned with their plates and set them down in front of the two detectives. "Saved by the bell," Stone said.

Cross grinned, showing his perfect set of teeth, and shook his head, saying, "No. It just postponed the inevitable, that's all."

Stone giggled and said, "Eat your burger."

After the pair finished eating, they paid and walked out to the parking lot. As they approached Stone's car, Cross said, "Man! That was a solid burger. I haven't had one that good in a long time."

Stone looked shocked and said, "Being a bodybuilder, I kinda figured you would be a health nut, not the burger and fries type."

Cross smiled and said, "There's a lot about me that will surprise you."

As the two got in Stone's unmarked car, she said, "Like what?"

"Like the fact that I used to be bullied as a kid because I was skinny. That's what got me into bodybuilding."

"NOOOO!" Stone exclaimed, "You used to get bullied because you were too small? That's hard to believe."

Cross smiled and said, "Yep, when I was little, my mama would say I could hide behind a string bean."

As Stone pulled out of the parking lot and headed back to the sheriff's office, she giggled and said, "Wow! That's hard to believe. What else should I know about Raylon Cross?"

Cross thought briefly, saying, "Well, you know about my nickname already. Let's see. I'm a crack shot with a pistol and grew up in the church. Now, back to you."

Trying to play it off, Stone said, "Back to me for what?"

Cross said, "Come on, I told you about me. It's your turn."

Stone sat there momentarily and smiled as if she were thinking about a good memory from her past. She said, "My dad was a cop, and that's why I became one over my mother's objections."

Suddenly, the tension in the car became so thick that it could be cut with a knife. Cross replied, "Hey, look, it's fine if you don't want to talk to me just yet, it's fine. I'm an open book. I don't mind telling you about myself. You tell me when you're ready."

As Stone pulled into the sheriff's department parking lot, she smiled and said, "Thanks. I appreciate it. It's just tough for me to talk about some things."

"I understand. You'll tell me when you're ready," Cross replied reassuringly. "Can I assume it has something to do with that tattoo with the black shamrock and the Veritas et Aequitas phrase on your arm?"

Stone smiled before they exited the car and said, "Yeah, it does. It means—"

"Truth and Justice," Cross replied before Stone could say it."

Stone smiled and said, "Exactly. How did you know that?"

Cross smiled and said, "I'm just that good. I can also tell you that, most often, the black shamrock signifies resistance. So, what are you resisting?"

Stone took a breath, shrugged, and replied, "The idea that my father's killer will most likely never be caught." Before Cross could respond or ask questions, Stone quickly hopped out of the car.

AFTER THE TWO got out of the car and went inside, Boone stopped them and asked how it was going. Before Stone could reply, Cross said, "As far as I'm concerned, it's great."

"Me too," Stone said with a forced smile.

"Glad to hear it. Somehow, I knew you two were going to work well together," Boone replied, smiling at Cross.

"What's that look for?" Stone said warily.

"No reason. I knew you two would be a great team. That's all," Boone reiterated. "Now get to work."

"We were on our way to the bullpen to get Cross set up with a desk when you stopped us," Stone replied.

Boone chuckled and said, "Ok, I can take a hint. Get to it."

Cross and Stone smiled and said, "See you later," before turning and walking off.

A few twists and turns later, the pair entered a large room with cubicles sectioning off the room. "Welcome to the bullpen," Stone said. "We just got the cubicle dividers recently. They were a welcome addition. It makes everything quieter. Come on, I'll show you our space."

"Nice. I like it already," Cross said with a smile. "Back home in Alabama, all we had was a large room and old beat-up desks."

Stone smiled and said, "Well, I'm sure we probably have a little better bankroll than the small department you came from."

"Yeah, true," Cross replied.

After several more twists and turns, Stone stopped at a cubicle shaped like a rectangle. It had two desks side by side and enough room for the detectives to walk behind them comfortably.

"Home sweet home," Stone replied.

"Man, this is great," Cross replied, "I could get used to this. This is bigger than my bedroom growing up, and I had to share it with two other brothers!"

Stone replied, "Well, that's good because we spend a lot of time in here. Do you have anything at home to bring for your desk?"

"I have a few things to make it feel more like home," Cross replied.

"Good," Stone replied.

Changing the subject, Cross asked, "So, around here, how long does it take for the coroner to get results?"

"Depending on the body and circumstances, it can take anywhere from a day to a week, sometimes more. I'm not sure about this body in particular. I have seen our coroner do a lot with less. So, there's hope anyway. With any luck, we will know something by in the morning."

Stone spent the next hour getting Cross set up with his computer access and ensuring the phone extension was now put in Cross' name instead of Clayton, her former partner.

Once everything was set up for Cross, the phone on Stone's desk began to ring. Stone picked up her phone and said, "Detective Stone."

"Hi, detective. This is Sandy at the front desk. I have a person on the phone who will not give his name but says he wants to speak to the lady detective. I'm unsure if he means you, but you're the only female detective available right now."

"Sure, I'll talk to him," Stone said. "Send the call to my desk," she replied before hanging up.

"What's up?" Cross asked.

"I'm not sure yet. Sandy at the front desk says somebody on the phone wants to speak to the lady detective. I'm not sure if it's me or not, but we'll find out soon. She's transferring the call to my desk now."

Momentarily, the phone on Stone's desk started ringing. Stone put it on speaker so Cross could also hear the conversation.

"This is Detective Stone. Who am I speaking with?"

Whispering, the man said, "Are you the lady detective who found the body on Goat Island?"

Stone looked at Cross, who pulled his phone out, turned on his dictate app, and set it by the phone. When she saw what Cross had done, she quietly gave him a thumbs-up sign. "Yes, that was me and my partner. Why? Do you have information for us?"

Ignoring the question, the man whispered, "What took you so long?"

"What do you mean?" Stone asked.

"I told you where to look! What took you so long?"

Stone glanced at Cross, who just shrugged his shoulders.

"What do you mean?"

"I told you where to go!" The voice snapped.

"How did you tell us? Maybe we missed it," Stone replied.

"Three weeks ago, I sent you something in the mail. There will be more. There has to be more. I'm sorry." The voice said, "Now that I know your name, keep an eye out."

They heard a click before Stone could say anything else, and the call abruptly ended.

"What in the hell?" Cross snapped.

"I don't know, but we're about to find out," Stone replied. She quickly stood up and said, "Bring your phone with you!"

The pair walked down to Boone's office, knocked, and barged in without waiting for a response. "Hey! What gives?" Boone snapped.

"First of all, I need a trace on my extension right now. We need to see where the last call to my extension originated from," Stone snapped. "Second, thanks to my fast-thinking partner, I have a recording for you to listen to that you won't believe."

Without even waiting for an explanation, Boone got on the phone, dialed a number, and said, "I need a trace on Detective Amy Stone's desk phone right now."

After Boone hung the phone up, Cross played the recording he made while Stone had the voice on the phone. After listening to the recording, Boone whistled and said, "Okay, I'm officially creeped out now. How about you two?"

Stone replied, "What bothers me is he was there today. He *knew* there was a lady detective on the scene."

"Yeah, that is kinda creepy," Cross admitted.

"But, I don't get the part when he said, I told you where to look. What did he mean by that?" Boone asked.

"I have no idea," Stone replied, shaking her head.

All three sat in silence for a moment until Cross said, "My take is this: according to the coroner, the body on the island has been there for around three weeks. The voice on the phone said he told you where to look. We can only assume that he meant where the body was located, which means he tried to get in contact with someone three weeks ago. The question is, what happened? What's different now than three weeks ago?"

The three sat silently for another moment while Stone and Boone wracked their brains until Stone snapped her fingers, breaking the silence and saying, "I've got it. Sandy was still on maternity leave."

Cross looked confused and asked, "Who's Sandy?"

Boone said, "Sandy is someone who doesn't get paid nearly enough. That's who she is."

Stone elaborated for Cross, stating, "Sandy is our front desk extraordinaire. She is amazing, and we're lucky to have her. She knows this place inside and out. If she can't answer a question, she can get you to the person who can answer that question. Well, it just so happens she returned from maternity leave two weeks ago."

"So, let's go to the front and talk to her," Cross replied, "Maybe she can help us figure out this mess."

As the two detectives stood up, Cross asked, "How long will it be before we find out anything on the trace to Stone's phone?"

Before Boone could answer, the phone on his desk rang, and he said, "About that long; hang on a minute."

Boone picked up the phone and said, "Boone here." Stone and Cross waited silently until Boone looked at them and shook his head from side to side. "Thanks," Boone said to the person on the phone and then hung up.

"What happened?" Cross asked.

"Whoever it was knows something about hiding his tracks. The caller used some internet connection and bounced it all over the place before getting to us. There was no way to track it."

"I figured that would be too easy," Stone said.

"How so?" Cross asked.

"My former partner and mentor, Detective Drew Clayton, always told me cases are never that easy."

"And he would be right, too," Cross replied.

"You two go see Sandy at the front desk. See what you can find out or if maybe she can point you in the right direction," Boone said.

Cross and Stone got up and walked through the maze of corridors to the front of the building where Sandy's desk is. Once they came out of the hallway and up beside her, Sandy said, "Hello, Detective Stone. This must be Detective Cross everyone has been talking about."

Raylon smiled brightly and said, "Yes, ma'am. I'm Detective Raylon Cross. What do you mean when you say everyone's been talking about me?"

"Nothing bad, just talk about how big you are and how nice you are, that's all."

"Thank you," Cross replied, "I hear you just came back from maternity leave."

Sandy beamed from ear to ear, saying, "I sure did." She took a newly framed photo off her desk and handed it to Cross so he could see her new baby.

Cross smiled brightly and said, "Aw, she's beautiful. What's her name?"

"Megan Kayla Johnston," Sandy replied, beaming.

Cross handed her the picture back and said, "I have a question for you. I know you were still on maternity leave three weeks ago. Is this right?"

"Yes," Sandy beamed.

Cross continued, "Do you have any mail or anything left over that came in while you were on maternity leave? Perhaps something still floating around here somewhere you didn't know what to do with?"

"No, detective. Why?"

Stone said, "That phone call we received a little while ago at my desk. The person said he sent us something in the mail three weeks ago while you were still out. We hoped something might still be around from when you were still on maternity leave."

"Sorry, but I haven't found anything like that. I am still in the process of putting my workspace back together as I like it, though, and I will be sure to keep a look out for you. If I find anything, you'll be the first to know."

Cross flashed another bright smile at Sandy and said, "Thank you. I would appreciate it."

As the two returned to their cubicle, Stone said, "Well, that was a bust."

"For now," Cross replied, "I guess the next thing is to see if we can identify the body."

5

For the rest of the day, Cross and Stone reviewed missing persons reports from two weeks to a month and a half in case the coroner was off by a little bit.

They narrowed it down to a few possible suspects, but they would not know for sure until they heard something from the coroner's office. Finally, the two detectives called it quits for the night, deciding they couldn't do much more until they heard from the coroner's office.

As Stone and Cross walked out to go home, Cross asked, "Wanna grab a beer to celebrate our first day together?"

"I'm a little tired, but I tell ya what, I'll go for one beer," Stone replied.

"Where do ya want to go?" Cross asked, "I still haven't found a good place to hang out around here."

"There is a place I go to occasionally," Stone replied. "Follow me."

With a simple nod, Cross went to his car and followed Stone turn by turn for a little over a mile until they got to a nearby bar and grill.

As soon as they walked in, the person behind the bar smiled and said, "Detective Stone! How are you doing?"

Stone smiled and said, "Doing ok," as she and Cross settled in at the bar.

The bartender asked, "Is this your new partner?"

"Sure is Tommy. The old man finally hung it up."

The bartender shook hands with Cross and replied, "Nice to meet you. Gotta be careful with this one. She's a handful."

Shaking hands with the bartender, Cross said, "I'm Raylon Cross, her new partner, and yeah, I know already."

"So, what can I get for you two tonight?" Tommy asked.

"Guinness for me," Stone said.

After Stone gave her order, the bartender looked at Cross, who said, "Yeah, sure, why not? Make that two of them."

"Coming right up," Tommy replied.

After the bartender walked off, Cross smirked and said, "That man called you by name. You don't just come here occasionally. Do you?"

"I do now. Let's say ... after my last breakup, I came here a little more than I should have."

"Fair enough," Cross replied, "Now, what's the story on the tattoo? Earlier, you said it was about your father."

Stone looked at Cross, took a deep breath, and said, "My father used to be on the job. He was a detective."

"He was killed on duty a number of years ago under somewhat mysterious circumstances, and his killer or killers have never been caught. I look into it in my spare time, ha ha, but I haven't found anything useful."

"That's terrible," Cross replied, "I'm sorry. I wouldn't have pushed so much if I had known, but it all makes sense now."

"What does?"

"That fire I see in your belly," Cross replied with his patented broad smile.

Moments later, the bartender returned with their beers. He sat them down in front of the detectives and asked if they needed anything else before he left to help other patrons. Neither needed anything else, so Tommy turned and walked off.

No sooner had the bartender turned his back, Cross picked up his beer and held it up to a light saying, "Damn! That's dark."

"Yeah, but it's good. Try it, or are you scared?" Stone asked with a devious smile.

Cross picked up the Guinness and took a big swig of the dark brown beer. After he set the beer down, he smiled and said, "That's actually good."

Stone smiled and said, "Now, what about you? Anything I need to know about you?"

"Nope, nothing at all. I'm an open book," Cross replied.

"Well, ok then," Stone replied as she drank her beer.

Once they finished their beers, they chatted for a few more minutes, and each went their separate ways for the night.

The following morning, after getting settled in at their desks, Stone called the Interim Coroner, Doctor Sandeep Singh, who was, for the time being, pulling double duty as the Interim and head coroner.

Stone put the call on the speaker so Cross could hear it and said, "Good morning, Dr. Singh. I have you on speakerphone with my partner, Detective Cross. I was calling to see if you could tell us anything else about the body recovered from Goat Island."

"Good morning, detectives. Although I can't give you a definitive timeline, I can tell you that my initial findings at the scene were correct. This person died around three weeks to a month ago."

"Dr. Singh, Cross here. Were you able to identify the body?"

"Unfortunately, no. I recovered DNA, which I ran through CODIS, but there were no hits, so it's a good indication that he's never been in any real trouble before, whoever he is. Considering the degradation of the fingers, there was no hope of getting fingerprints."

"So, we still have nothing?" Cross asked.

"Not exactly," Singh replied, "Upon X-raying the remains, I discovered this individual had a plate placed in his right forearm on his radius bone, most likely due to a fracture earlier in life. These plates are serialized and could provide me with an identification. I will let you know when I have something. Is there anything else?"

"Yes, doctor," Stone replied, "Were you able to determine the manner of death?"

"At this point, what I can tell you is that there were what appeared to be two stab wounds to the victim's right side directly between the ribs, which killed the victim almost immediately," Singh replied.

"Okay, thank you, doctor," Stone replied.

As soon as Stone hung up the phone with Dr. Singh, Cross couldn't resist poking a little fun at Singh and said in a proper tone, "He sure is a well-spoken fellow, isn't he, Detective Stone?"

Stone giggled and said, "Yeah, he is, but he's really good at what he does."

The pair had just hung up with Dr. Singh when Stone's desk phone started ringing. Stone answered the phone, saying, "Detective Stone here." Cross listened intently for a moment, and then Stone said, "We'll be right up."

After hanging up the phone, Stone said, "That was Sandy at the front desk. She said she found something strange in her desk that apparently came in the mail while she was gone."

They left their cubicle and walked up front to Sandy's desk. As they approached her desk, Stone said, "Hey, Sandy. What did you find?"

"Well, I don't know, exactly," Sandy replied. I finally got around to cleaning out all my desk drawers and getting them as I had them before I went on maternity leave. Anyway, I found this."

Sandy handed Detective Stone a small envelope with the word Detectives typed on the outside in an old typewriter-style font.

"What is it?" Cross asked.

"I have no idea," Sandy replied. "I just found it mixed in with other stuff in one of my desk drawers that I use for supplies. There was no exterior envelope or anything. I found it just like that. I've never seen it before, so I have no idea how long it's been here."

"Thank you," Stone said as she pulled on a pair of latex gloves that she always had on her and gently opened the envelope. Squeezing each end of the envelope slightly, Stone glanced inside and could see what appeared to be a piece of paper about the size of a business card with nothing more than a QR code on the front.

Stone tilted the envelope so Cross could see what was inside. Then she thanked Sandy, and they headed back to their cubicle. On their way back, Cross asked, "You don't think this is what the caller meant, do you?"

"There's only one way to find out," Stone said as they rounded the corner and stepped back into their work area. Cross watched as Stone placed the envelope on her desk.

Stone walked over to the copier and gently took the piece of paper out of the envelope by one corner. She made a photocopy of both sides of the paper and the envelope ensuring the preservation of the original to be processed as evidence. Before they processed it, they both noticed there was nothing on the back of the slip of paper. On the front was a QR code with no wording at all.

Stone gently laid the slip of paper on the desk and took her phone out. After turning on the camera on her phone, she hovered the phone over the mysterious QR code on the paper, and an odd-looking web address appeared.

Stone clicked on the web address, opening a simple web page quickly. The web page contained a string of numbers separated by a space.

Below the string of numbers was the phrase,

I am Legion

Cross looked at the screen and said, "Oh, shit."

"What is it? Do you recognize it?"

"Yeah, I do, and it's not good," Cross replied.

"Spill it," Stone replied.

"It's from the Bible. In the Gospel of Mark, Jesus got into a boat and went across a sea or, in some scriptures … a lake. Either way, he went to a region called the Gerasenes. According to scripture, he was approached by a man with an impure spirit or demon when he got there—"

Stone cut Cross off, asking," What does a biblical reference have to do with this?"

"Patience, Grasshopper," Cross replied, as he recited a famous line from the television series Kung Fu, "I'm getting there. When Jesus arrived, the man ran over to him and fell on his knees in front of him, begging Jesus not to torture him. Jesus replied, "Come out of this man, you impure spirit!"

"I still don't get it," Stone replied.

Ignoring Stone, Cross continued, "Jesus asked, what is your name?"

After that, he paused momentarily, and just as he wanted, Stone asked, "Well, what did the man say?"

Cross said, "My name is Legion, for we are many."

Stone paused a moment and repeated Cross' statement, "Oh, shit is right ... I'm almost scared to ask, but what happened?"

Cross replied, "Jesus commanded the demons to come out. The demons begged Jesus not to make them leave the area. Instead, a large herd of pigs was feeding on a nearby hillside. The demons begged Jesus to let them go into the pigs. He gave them permission, and after they went into the pigs, they ran down a steep bank into the lake and drowned."

Stone sat there in silence for a moment, then said, "So, this guy is off his rocker, or he's becoming a serial killer."

"Possibly," Cross replied, "but with just one body; we can't say that yet for sure, although ... he is taunting us as a serial would."

"No, but we need to talk to Boone anyway," Stone replied as she picked up the phone and called their boss, Chief of Detectives Boone, to tell him they needed to talk. Before Boone arrived, Stone asked, "So, tell me, how is it that you know about this Legion from the Bible?"

Cross replied, "I grew up in the church. Remember?"

Stone smiled and said, "You're a well-rounded man, aren't you?"

Cross flashed one of his patented smiles and said, "You could say that."

A few minutes later, Boone rounded the corner to their cubicle and asked, "What's going on?"

Stone and Cross informed Boone about what had happened with the envelope so far, and then they showed Boone what the QR code did when they scanned it. Boone looked at the string of numbers and said, "If I'm not mistaken, those very well could be GPS coordinates. Have you tried looking them up to see?"

"Not yet. We just scanned the QR code right before we called you."

"Give it a shot to see what happens," Boone replied. "Copy and paste both sets of numbers into Google. If they are GPS coordinates, it should open maps and show you where it is."

Cross and Boone watched over Stone's shoulder as she did what Boone said. When she clicked enter on Google, the coordinates took her directly to Goat Island, where the body was located. "Well, I'll be damned!" Stone said, shocked.

When Stone hit the enter key on her keyboard, the screen centered dead-on Goat Island. In the center of the island was the pin showing the location of the coordinates. "If I'm not mistaken, that's right about where the body was found," Cross said.

"Sure looks like it," Stone said. Suddenly, she snapped her fingers and said, "That's what he meant when he said, "I told you where to go! He's remorseful for what he did!"

Just then, the phone on Stone's desk began to ring. Picking it up, Stone said, "This is Detective Stone," both Boone and Cross listened intently as Stone said, "He's on *now*! Yes, transfer him, please."

Before she even hung up, Boone asked, "What's going on?"

"That was Sandy at the front desk. The caller is on the line right now. She is getting ready to transfer him to me now. Cross, get your phone out to record like last time."

Seconds later, Stone's desk phone started ringing. Once Cross was ready and gave Stone the thumbs up, she picked up the phone and put it directly on the speaker's phone.

"This is Detective Stone. We found your note. It had gotten lost. Legion, is that your name?"

Finally, the voice answered in a whisper like before, saying, "You may call me that. Do you know who he is yet?"

"Actually, no. Since it took us so long to find the body, our coroner is having trouble identifying him. Can you help us with that? He deserves a decent burial, and his relatives deserve to know what happened to him."

"Then you need to find out who he was," the voice whispered.

While Stone was talking to the voice on the phone, Boone called the tech guys and once again had them start tracing the phone call. "We can't. The body was too far gone to determine who he was as of now. Tell me who he was," Stone pleaded.

After a slight pause, the voice whispered, "I can't. I don't know who he was, but I will tell you this ... I took him from the boat in the lake a few weeks ago."

Before Stone could ask anything else, the line went dead with an audible click.

"Damn!" Stone snapped as she slammed her phone down. "I almost had him."

Before anyone could say anything else, Boone's cell phone rang, and Stone and Cross heard him say, "Thanks for trying," before hanging up.

"I take it you didn't get a trace," Cross huffed.

"No, but Stone got us enough. I know how we can figure out how to identify the body without having to wait for the coroner."

"How's that?" Cross asked.

Boone replied, "About a month ago, a fishing boat was found adrift in the lake well before you arrived. It was assumed the person fell overboard and drowned because no remains were ever found. What if the body on Goat Island is indeed the missing fisherman?"

Stone said, "That would explain why we couldn't find a record of anything in Lexington County. It seems like he went missing from an Airbnb in Saluda County. Saluda County took the lead, our dive team assisted, but nothing was ever found."

Before Boone returned to his desk, he said, "I'd suggest calling over to the Saluda County Sheriff's Office and talking to their detectives. Maybe they can help."

"Will do," Cross replied as Boone disappeared out of sight.

DETECTIVE STONE MADE the phone call and talked about the case for twenty minutes or more with one of the Saluda County Sheriff's Detectives. After chatting with him, Stone discovered that the missing boater's name was Jeramy Donahue from Charlotte, North Carolina.

Once Stone had that information, she pulled up his DMV photo and sent a copy of it to Doctor Singh in the coroner's office to see if they could get a positive identification on their victim.

Not long after Stone forwarded the information to the interim Coroner, Doctor Singh, her phone rang. Both Stone and Cross paused momentarily, thinking there was no way Dr. Singh could get a positive match that quickly.

Stone picked up the phone, and before she could utter a word, Sandy at the front desk blurted out, "You have another envelope like the previous one!"

"Don't touch it! We'll be right there!" Stone nearly shouted.

Both Stone and Cross lept out of their chairs, grabbed rubber gloves, and took off to the front where Sandy worked.

As soon as they arrived at Sandy's desk, Cross and Stone both saw the envelope sitting right on the top of the stack of mail that the mail carrier had just dropped off. Neither Cross nor Stone were too careful with the first envelope because it had been moved around quite a bit, but they were much more cautious this time.

Before moving it, they called for a crime scene technician to meet them in the lobby. The technician carefully removed the envelope from Sandy's desk and took it for processing. Stone and Cross followed the technician to the lab and watched him photocopy both sides of the envelope. Then, with the precision of a surgeon, the technician opened the envelope, reached inside with a pair of tweezers, and gently pulled out the slip of paper that was inside which was also photocopied.

The technician then closely examined the stamp on the envelope. Cross said, "Please tell me you can pull DNA off that stamp."

After carefully working his magic, the technician replied, "Sadly, no, it's a self-adhesive stamp."

Stone and Cross watched as the technician sprayed the envelope with Ninhydrin and ran a steam iron over its exterior. Several areas of the envelope turned magenta, but no usable fingerprints were found.

Again, the slip of paper inside held a QR code and nothing more. Before the technician dusted it for fingerprints using magnetic fingerprint powder, Stone scanned the QR code with her phone, and just like before, a simple webpage opened, showing another set of coordinates. On the second line of the webpage was another phrase that read:

May his soul find peace, even if mine never will.

While Stone left the webpage with the coordinates on her phone, Cross typed the coordinates into Google, hit the enter key, and held his breath for the results.

6

Cross watched as the map on his phone changed. "Aw, shit!" Cross said in disgust.

"What is it?" Stone asked.

"Those coordinates are on another island in the lake," Cross replied disheartened.

"That's not good ... not good at all," Stone replied, knowing full well what the implications are. "Which island?"

"How should I know?" Cross replied, "Take a look for yourself."

Cross handed Stone his phone, and she was obviously unhappy with what she saw. "Damn!"

"What is it?" Cross asked.

"That's Bomb Island, and it's right smack in the middle of the lake."

Cross' eyes widened, and he said, "Uh, wait a minute, I think I blanked out after hearing the word bomb. What do you mean when you say ... bomb?"

Stone smiled and said, "Not what you think. During World War II, the US Army Air Corps used the island for training purposes. Ever heard of the Doolittle raid on Japan?"

"Yeah, sure I have," Cross replied.

"Well, they secretly trained here. The Columbia Metropolitan Airport started off as a US Army airfield. The Doolittle Raiders trained here for a while. Anyway, bombers would leave from the airfield, fly over the lake, and drop practice bombs filled with white sand on the island.

"White sand?" Cross asked.

"Yep, when the casings hit and broke on contact with the ground, which is mostly red clay, the contrast between the white sand and the red clay would mimic a puff of smoke to the bombers, indicating a hit."

Cross breathed a sigh of relief and said, "So, no live bombs then?"

"Nope, no live bombs," Stone said. "Come on, we gotta tell Boone." Before leaving the lab, Stone told the technician, "I doubt you're going to find anything, but if you get a print or any DNA, I want to know about it."

"Don't worry, I'll call you whether or not I find anything," the technician replied.

Afterward, the pair went to tell Chief of Detectives Boone about the new note in the mail. After they filled in Boone, he asked, "Same QR code and basic webpage?"

"Identical," Cross replied.

Boone asked warily, "Where are the coordinates?"

Stone took a deep breath and said, "Bomb Island."

"Crap!" Boone replied, "I'm starting to really not like this case."

"You and me both," Stone replied.

Boone thought momentarily and replied, "All right, you two get going towards the lake. I'll call you while you're en route with the meet-up location for one of our boats."

"Just so I'm clear, a Lexington County Sheriff's boat, correct?" Cross asked."

"That's the plan for now. Why?" Boone asked.

Cross smiled deviously and replied, "Oh, no reason."

"Well, okay then. Get going," Boone snapped.

Cross and Stone grabbed some radios and headed to Stone's car. Not five minutes after pulling out from the sheriff's department,

Stone's phone rang. Stone pulled the phone from the clip on her belt, hit the speakerphone button, and said, "Stone here. I have you on speaker with Cross. What's up, Chief?"

"Good news, bad news," Boone replied.

"Give us the good news," Stone said.

"Okay, the good news is I have arranged for a boat to pick you up at the same boat ramp by number six, just like before," Boone replied.

"Okay, so what's the bad news?" Cross asked.

Boone paused and said, "Our boats have been called away for something else. So, that means you'll have to hitch a ride over on a SCDNR boat."

Cross said, "Somehow, I have a sneaky suspicion that I know who will be there to take us to the coordinates."

"Well, if you are talking about Russell Watts, you would be correct, Detective Cross," Boone replied. I have been assured by DNR HQ that Watts is one of the best, if not the best, officer on the lake."

"Lovely," Cross replied.

When the two detectives pulled into the parking lot at the boat ramp where Highway Six intersects with Bush River Road, they saw the SCDNR boat waiting at the dock.

Stone parked, and as both detectives walked out onto the dock where the SCDNR boat was tied up, Watts, sitting in the driver's seat, said, "It's like fate that we're supposed to be together ... The Three Amigos! Back together again!"

Cross asked in a monotone voice, "Can I hurt him?"

Stone playfully smacked Cross on the shoulder and said, "Uh, that would be a no. I can't have my partner getting into trouble on his second day on the job."

Both detectives hopped aboard, put on their life jackets, and took the same seats they had previously taken on the ride to Goat Island. Once everyone was ready, Watts untied the boat and slowly backed away from the dock. The trio made the twenty-five-minute journey to Bomb Island, located near the center of the lake.

As soon as they arrived on the island, Watts slowed the boat and began circling it to reach a small strip of beach he knew was on the opposite side of the island. As he slowly motored around, Cross asked, "What's up with the birds hanging around?"

Watts replied, "Purple Martins. They are migrating south from up north and Canada. These birds are a little early. This is nothing. In the summer, they come here by the tens of thousands. People know the island is off limits during the summer months while the Purple Martins are here, so they anchor offshore to watch the birds return."

"That's crazy," Cross said. "Where do they go once they leave here?"

Watts replied, "I know of one tagged over a year ago, and it was tracked for quite a while. It started in Canada, traveled south, where it stayed at Bomb Island for the summer, and then continued south until it reached South America. The last time it was located was in the Brazilian rainforest."

"That's crazy," Cross replied as Watts found the landing spot he had been looking for.

Within a few minutes, all three stood on the island's edge in knee-deep scrub brush while Stone pulled up the coordinates on the hand-held GPS she procured from Boone before leaving the department. "You guys go ahead, I gotta make sure the boat is secure," Watts said. "I'll catch up."

Before leaving the shore, Stone said, "It shouldn't be too far to the coordinates as long as we don't have to make any detours for anything."

"We won't have to," Watts replied confidently. I've been over most of this island, and for the most part, it's flat. The only thing is that there are some dense patches of trees and brush, but it's nothing to worry about."

"Good," Stone said with a slight smile, impressed with Watts' knowledge of the island.

Cross, who was keeping a wary eye on Watts, huffed, "Can we get going, please? I don't want to be out here all day."

Stone let out a little chuckle and said, "We're heading out now."

Stone and Cross navigated through Bomb Island's interior for fifteen minutes until Stone stopped and said, "Okay, according to the GPS, we're at the coordinates. Let's fan out and start looking around."

By that time, Watts had caught up to them, and not five minutes after starting to search the area, Cross shouted, "I've got a body!"

Stone and Watts converged on Cross's location, careful not to disturb anything. Just as with the first body, this body was posed with his arms across his chest precisely as the first. The only difference was that this body was almost perfectly intact.

Cross, who was kneeling near the remains, said as the other two came into view, "He couldn't have been here more than a day or two at most."

"Damn!" Stone snapped, "I was hoping for a clue ... but not this."

"Who ... who would do such a thing?" Watts asked.

"A seriously deranged person," Cross replied as he stared at the body of a young man who had obviously been deceased before he was dumped out here.

"At least this body is in much better shape than the previous body," Cross said.

Stone thought momentarily and said, "Yeah, it's as if he wants us or needs us to find the bodies quickly. The question is, why?"

"And this is why I became a game warden," Watts replied, "I don't have to deal with these kinds of unpleasant situations."

Ignoring Watts' statement, Cross replied, "Remember the recordings? He's remorseful. He doesn't want to do these killings, but he feels like he has to for some unknown reason. He's compelled to do it. That's why he wants us to find the bodies quickly. He doesn't want them to be out here longer than necessary."

Stone smiled and said, "I think you're on to something, partner. Let's call the calvary."

Stone and Cross tried to get a signal but could not get enough bars to make a call. Watts suggested, "If you go back to the boat, you'll find you have a signal. It's wide open ... these trees and brush are just enough to mess with a signal this far out."

Cross looked back and forth warily between Stone and Watts,

then uttered to Stone, "I'll be back as soon as I can. If he tries something, shoot him."

Stone laughed and said, "I believe I'll be all right."

Cross cautiously retraced the same path the three had taken to find the body so he could get back closer to the lake and hopefully get enough of a signal to call out. As luck would have it, he managed to get to the island's edge within sight of the boat, having only missed the mark by fifteen or twenty yards.

As soon as Cross saw the boat, though, he realized something was wrong. The boat sat much lower in the stern than when they arrived. Speeding up somewhat, Cross jogged the rest of the way to the boat to find it was taking on water.

About that time, Cross heard three distinct gunshots emanating from the island's interior. After hearing the gunshots, Cross' eyes widened, and although alone, he snapped, "I hope she knows I was joking! I didn't really mean to shoot the guy!"

Immediately, Cross drew his service weapon and ran headlong in the direction the shots came from. Slowing as he got back to the area where he last saw Stone and Watts, he started methodically checking his surroundings. He moved cautiously until he spotted both Stone and Watts crouched behind two nearby trees.

Sliding up beside Stone, Cross said, "I can't leave you alone for ten minutes. Can I? What in the hell is going on?"

Stone pointed at Watts, behind a nearby tree, and said, "John Wayne over there said somebody was watching us. He said he saw the person reach around like he was reaching into the small of his back for a weapon, so he fired three rounds. After that, the guy took off running. I never saw anything, but I thought I heard something running off through the woods."

Cross giggled and said, "Geeze, for a split second when I was back at the boat, I thought you may have actually shot him."

Stone replied, "He's cute, but I'm not about to lose my job over the likes of him."

Cross smiled and said, "You don't know how happy that makes me to hear that."

All three remained behind cover for another minute until they heard the sound of a nearby boat racing away from the island. "What do you want to bet that the person we just scared off was somehow tied to the murders?" Stone asked.

"No bet," Watts replied as all three cautiously stood up and holstered their weapons.

Stone looked at Cross and asked, "Were you able to get a call out?"

"Not yet. I had just arrived back at the boat when I heard the gunshots and came sprinting back."

Watts replied, "If we can get back to the boat quickly enough, we can see which direction he went, and with a little luck, we can get close enough to get a description and a registration number off the boat."

Cross paused momentarily and said, "Yeah ... about that."

Watts stared at Cross and asked, "What is it? He didn't hurt my baby. Did he?"

"Well, let's just say we're not going anywhere anytime soon," Cross replied with an evil grin.

"What?" Watts exclaimed, horrified, before tearing off to the water's edge where they had left the boat.

"Are we stuck here on this island?" Stone asked.

"Sure looks like it," Cross replied. "Meanwhile, our first and only lead is tearing off across the lake as we speak while we sit here on this chunk of rock in the middle of the lake."

Stone and Cross followed Watts to where they had come ashore to find the boat's stern sitting low in the water and possibly on the bottom of the lake already. As Stone and Cross arrived at the water's edge, where Watts was standing, he put his hands on top of his head in disgust and said, "The boss is going to kill me!"

"More importantly, now what do we do?" Cross asked.

Without directly answering Cross, Stone took her phone out and called Chief of Detectives Boone to let him know what was happening. After hanging up with Boone, Stone said sarcastically, "That went well. The boss could not believe we were on the island with the probable killer, and we let him get away."

"How bad was it?" Cross asked.

"There were some expletives thrown around, and he couldn't believe how two armed detectives and supposedly one of the best game wardens on the lake could let this happen. He'll be ok, though. He's sending the cavalry to us as we speak."

About that time, Watts walked up and said, "My turn. I gotta call my boss. I want him to hear this from me and not your boss."

Stone giggled and said, "I think you're a little late."

Before Watts could even ask, his phone started ringing. As he answered, he walked a short distance away so Stone and Cross couldn't hear what was being said. However, with Watts' body language, they knew it wasn't good.

"Poor guy," Stone said.

"Yeah, my heart breaks for him," Cross replied.

Not long after that, a beautiful 23-foot Premier Sensation pontoon boat appeared from around the opposite side of the island. All three waved their hands to grab the boat captain's attention.

Several people on board the pontoon boat furiously waved back to assure the stranded trio they had been seen and that help was coming. Watts was ready and waiting as the captain's pontoon boat bumped ashore.

From the pontoon boat console, the captain asked his passengers to stay seated momentarily. Then he walked up to the bow to help Watts get aboard while Stone and Cross stayed on shore: "I'm Captain Wade Campbell, owner of Top Tier Charters. Is everybody okay?"

"Yeah, we're good," Watts replied, "just a little thirsty. Do you happen to have any water?"

Campbell went to a cooler, grabbed three bottles of ice-cold water, and handed them to Watts.

"What happened?" Campbell asked innocently.

"Long story, but in short, we were sabotaged. You didn't happen to see a boat tearing out of here a little while ago, did you?"

"I saw one from a distance headed away from the island at a pretty good clip. Is he the one who did this to your boat?"

"Yeah, we believe so. Were you able to see any details or get a registration number by chance?"

Campbell shook his head and said, "No, he was too far away. The only thing I can tell you about the boat is that it was a white center console boat, several years old. They're a dime a dozen on the lake."

"Figured as much," Watts replied disheartened.

"I was coming around the island to set an anchor so the folks on my charter could start bird watching and taking pictures when I saw your boat sitting low in the water. You guys want to hop aboard and watch the Purple Martins return to roost with us?"

"Yeah!" replied the kids and their parents, who'd rented the charter. Because they were eager to have real detectives and a game warden aboard.

Smiling, Watts replied, "We would love to, but we have to stay near the shore now. I can't exactly say why, though. I have already called it in, and help should be arriving soon, but thank you for the water, though."

"Not a problem. Take a few extras, just in case," Campbell replied.

Watts tossed bottles of cold water to Cross and Stone onshore, who promptly drank half of their bottles at once. Watts lept ashore, turned, and thanked Campbell, who tossed them another water bottle. Campbell said, "I'm going to back off the island a hundred yards or so, but we will be in the area for a while, and I will stop by before I leave to make sure you guys are ok."

"Thank you. We appreciate the help," Watts replied.

The trio watched as Captain Wade expertly backed his pontoon boat away from the restricted island and anchored not far away so his charter could see the Purple Martins return when the time came.

With nothing else to do, Stone and Cross returned to the body dump while Watts stayed near his now-swamped boat and waited for help to arrive.

∾

AFTER ARRIVING BACK at the body dump, Cross and Stone got as close as they dared, and then each pulled out a set of rubber gloves they had in their pockets and put them on.

Stone knelt beside the body, and that's when she noticed a piece of paper sticking out of his right front pocket. Stone slowly and ever so carefully started to reach for the piece of paper when Cross said, "Wait a minute. I know I'm new here, but isn't the coroner supposed to go through the victim's pockets?"

"Technically speaking, yes," Stone replied as she ever-so-gently pulled the paper from the victim's pocket, looked at Cross, and smiled, saying, "But this was not in his pocket."

"So, what does it say now that you have broken protocol?" Cross asked.

Stone carefully unfolded the small piece of paper, looked it over, and said, "It's a receipt from two nights ago."

Cross replied, "I'm almost scared to ask, but where from?"

"Oddly enough, it's from The Palms Grill & Bar in Newberry."

"Newberry? Where in the hell is that?" Cross asked.

Shocked, Stone replied, "It's a small town up the interstate about twenty-five miles away, give or take a mile or two."

"Great," Cross huffed. "So, this guy is moving around. It's going to be much more difficult to catch him."

"That's just what I was thinking," Stone replied.

About that time, Watts returned to where Cross and Stone were located and said, "The calvary's here ... it looks like one of your boats and two of mine are here."

"Excellent," Stone replied.

Before long, Bomb Island, home to tens of thousands of Purple Martins, was now also ground zero for the next body dump.

7

It took several hours for Watts and his cohorts to make emergency repairs to the three-inch gash in his boat, which he surmised was created by a hatchet, and to pump the water out. Ultimately, they got his boat re-floated and towed it back to the nearest marina, where they could get it out of the water.

While DNR attempted to salvage and recover Watts' boat scarcely yards offshore, Dr. Singh, crime scene technicians, and photographers worked diligently on the island's interior, processing the dump site and the body.

Before Dr. Singh left with the body, Stone and Cross stopped him, and Stone asked, "So, what do you think, Dr. Singh?"

Dr. Singh paused a moment and replied, "First of all, I'm not happy about you breaking protocol and going inside the victim's pockets as you did ... however, it looks like he's only been dead for a day, perhaps two at the most."

"Technically speaking, we didn't go inside his pockets," Stone replied. "The receipt was sticking out, and I just pulled it the rest of the way out."

"Don't try to get cute with me, detective. You know you are supposed to wait for the coroner to do anything like that. You could have compromised the body or the scene, and my report will reflect that," Dr. Singh scolded.

"I completely understand. Now, back to the body, if you please," Stone replied, unfazed by Dr. Singh's words.

Singh replied, "Very well ... this individual has two apparent stab wounds to the right side between the ribs, very similar to the previous body. I won't know for certain until I get the body back to the morgue, but it is my supposition that the same person killed both this and the previous victim."

"Age?" Cross asked.

Singh paused momentarily and replied, "Judging by his appearance and greying colored hair, my best guess is approximately mid to late fifties."

After Dr. Singh's people secured the body and moved it aboard a Lexington County Sheriff's boat and all the crime scene technicians had finished their work, the island was once again returned to the Purple Martins.

With Watts gone and having to be towed back due to the damage to his boat, Cross and Stone hitched a ride back on a sheriff's boat, which was okay with Cross because it meant he didn't have to keep an eye on Watts with his new partner.

Hours later, Stone and Cross were finally back at the boat ramp where they had met Watts earlier in the day. As they walked up the short dock to Stone's vehicle, Stone said, "Man, what a day. I can't wait to get in the car and turn on the AC. I'm dying from being in the sun all day."

Cross smiled and said, "I know what you mean. It's been a rough one." As the two approached the car, they saw a slip of paper under the driver's side windshield wiper. Without thinking about it, Stone grabbed the slip of paper, unfolded it, and skimmed over it.

Stone paused a moment to read, and before Cross could ask, "Stone said, "SON OF A BITCH!"

"What is it?" Cross asked.

Without saying, Stone handed Cross the printed note that read, *thank you*

"I guess it's safe to assume there are no cameras in the parking lot. Are there?" Cross asked.

"Nope. So, this guy, knowing we're stuck out there on the island all day, apparently comes here and leaves this on my car. Why?" Stone asked.

"More importantly, how did he know to come here and put a note on your unmarked car?" Cross asked.

"When he made contact the first time, he knew we were at the first crime scene on Goat Island. I guess it's possible he followed us back here, and we didn't notice it."

Cross looked around momentarily and spotted a man fishing on the shore nearby. "Hang on a second," Cross said.

Ready to go, Stone replied, "Come on, let's get out of here."

"Patience, grasshopper," Cross replied as he walked toward the man fishing on the bank.

"Shit," Stone mumbled as she watched Cross walk off.

The middle-aged man fishing on the shore glanced over his shoulder as Cross approached. He quickly started gathering his gear and reeling in the line he had in the water.

"Easy there, I'm not a game warden," Cross said with his patented smile. "I don't care if you don't have a fishing license."

"You got a gun and a badge, though. Whadda ya want with me?"

"I need to ask you a couple of questions, and I'll let you get back to fishing," Cross replied.

"What kind of questions?" the man asked.

"Well, for starters, how long have you been here today?"

The man paused momentarily and replied, "Got here 'bout ten this morning."

"Have you seen anything ... unusual while you've been here?" Cross asked.

"If you're asking if I saw somebody pull up in a boat and walk into the parking lot, then leave again ... the answer is yeah. I saw him."

"Great! Could you tell me what he looked like?"

"Not really. He was not that close, and I was watching my line. White guy, about a six-footer, maybe more. He had brown hair, though."

"Did you, by any chance, see where he went or what kind of boat he was in?"

"Naw, all I saw was him tie his boat up real quick like, run into the parking lot and run right back. He was here ... five minutes at most. As far as the boat, it was a white boat with a center console and a few fishing rods."

"Beautiful," Cross replied, smiling. You wouldn't happen to have noticed a registration number on the boat, would you?"

"Naw, sorry." The fisherman replied.

"That's fine. You did great. Thank you," Cross replied before rapidly walking back to the car.

As Cross approached Stone, who was still standing beside the car, Stone asked, "So, did he see anything?"

"Tell ya in the car, but first, let's fire this thing up and get some AC going."

As Stone cranked the car, Cross reached up, turned the AC wide open, and said, "Ahh, that's better!"

On the way back to the sheriff's department, Stone asked, "So, did the old fisherman see anything?"

"Yeah, it was our guy, for sure. The old guy said he saw a white guy with brown hair pull up to the dock, tie his boat up, and run into the parking lot. He was here for maybe five minutes."

"Just enough time to leave a note on my car," Stone said.

"Exactly, and it was a center console fishing type of boat, which is basically what the charter boat captain told us."

"This is getting a little too close to home," Cross replied.

"Aw, is the big man scared of the serial killer?" Stone chided.

"I'm not the one he wants to talk to. You are," Cross reminded her.

"Any chance we can stop at a pharmacy on the way back to the department?"

"Sure. You good?"

"Yeah, I just want to grab some things to keep in my desk so I can freshen up when we get back," Cross replied.

"Not a problem," Stone said. "That's actually not a bad idea."

After their stop, the duo spent the rest of the ride back to the department in silence, no doubt thinking about the case wondering who may have been doing these killings, and why.

After freshening up in their respective locker rooms, both met back at their shared cubicles to strategize about their next move, but Chief Boone had other plans.

Boone was waiting for them when they returned to their cubicle, and as soon as they rounded the corner, Boone said, "Sounds like you two had a hell of a day."

"We sure did," Stone answered.

"Okay, get me caught up," Boone replied.

For the next ten minutes, Stone and Cross filled Boone in on the day's events, the body, and the receipt hanging out of the pocket. "By the way, about that—" Stone started to say before being cut off mid-sentence.

"Save it," Boone replied. I've already received a call from Singh asking me to remind you of the particulars of crime scene etiquette, as he put it ... don't worry about it. I would have done the same thing. Now, you two finish up and get out of here for the night. You've had a long day. Start fresh in the morning."

"Yes sir," Cross replied as he turned the light off on his desk and stood up. After Boone left and Cross saw that Stone wasn't getting up to leave, he asked, "You're not leaving, are you?"

"Nope, I want to check a few more things before I go," Stone replied.

After hearing Stone's reply, Cross sat down and said, "If you're not leaving, I'm not leaving either. What can I do?"

Stone asked, "You any good with computers?"

"Fairly good. Why?" Cross asked.

"Do you think you can find out anything about the websites the killer is using?"

"I can sure try," Cross said with a wink and a smile. "What are you going to be doing?"

"I will be going over everything we know so far about the case," Stone replied, "which admittedly isn't much."

The next thing both realized was that it was well past seven thirty at night, and they were spinning their wheels, getting nowhere.

They decided to call it a night and start fresh in the morning with rested eyes. They already knew they were going to the Palms Grill and Bar in Newberry to talk with them about the receipt in the last victim's pocket. Hopefully, it would point them to another lead and, with any luck, the second victim's identity.

Little did they know that come the following morning, everything would change ...

8

T he next morning, Stone walked into the room affectionately called the bullpen and through the maze of cubicles until she got to her and Cross' elongated cubicle. As she turned the corner with two coffees, Stone was surprised to see Cross sitting at his desk, already reviewing some of yesterday's papers.

"You're here already," Stone said as she handed him a coffee cup and a small paper bag of creamers and sugar packets. "Sorry, I didn't know how you like your coffee."

Cross thanked Stone for the coffee and said, "Just a little milk or cream to cut the acid," Cross replied before taking a sip.

"Easy enough," Stone replied, grinning. "My old partner always taught me that any detective worth his or her salt never forgets when it's their turn to get coffee."

"And he was right, too," Cross replied.

"So, what are you up to already?" Stone asked.

"Nothing much, just going over some notes, that's all."

"Find anything?" Stone asked.

"Not a thing," Cross replied, shaking his head.

Before Stone could say anything else, both heard, "Good morning, amigos!"

Both Cross and Stone turned towards the entrance of their cubicle to see SCDNR Game Warden Russell Watts standing there with a big smile on his face. "It was until you showed up. What in the hell are you doing here?" Cross grumbled.

"You mean you don't know either?" Watts asked.

"No, we just got here a few minutes ago," Stone replied.

"I figured you would know what's going on if anybody would. I was just told to come here this morning since my baby is still being fixed up from being sabotaged yesterday."

"Great, just great!" Cross snapped. "I haven't been here a week yet, and we're already in trouble."

"Somebody's grumpy in the mornings, aren't they?" Watts said, goading Cross.

Stone smiled and said, "Hang on, don't jump the gun there, big man. We haven't done anything."

"Oh, no? "Cross asked, "What about letting the best lead we've had yet slip through our fingers yesterday?"

Before Stone could say anything, Watts said obviously messing with Cross, "You got a point. You kinda did let him get away."

"You were *that* kid, weren't you?" Stone asked.

"What do you mean?" Watts asked.

"You were the kind of kid growing up that always had to be told to keep your hands to yourself or stop aggravating other people, weren't you?" Stone asked.

"What gave it away?" Watts asked innocently.

"I have no idea," Stone said as she rolled her eyes at him.

Just then, the phone on Stone's desk rang. She picked it up and said, "This is Detective Stone ... we will be right there ... Watts, too, yes, sir."

"So, what was that about?" Cross asked.

Stone said, "Boone wants to see all of us in the conference room right away."

Cross replied, "Somehow, I just know this day is gonna suck."

Stone smiled, patted Cross on the shoulder, and said, "Think of it as another opportunity to catch our killer leaving those bodies on those islands in the lake."

Stone led Cross and now Watts to a large conference room with several tables and a whiteboard on one wall.

As soon as they walked in, Boone's boss, Undersheriff Nicholas Reed, stood at the front by the whiteboard with the name of the first victim and the words *victim two* beside that. A couple of other people were already seated at the front table. When the three walked in, Reed said, "And here they are now."

Everyone in the room turned to look at them, and as soon as one of the individuals turned around, Stone locked eyes with him and softly said, "Oh, shit!"

"Who is that?" Cross asked.

Stone paused momentarily and replied, "None other than Peter Davenport ... my ex," Stone replied under her breath.

Cross thought for a moment, then his eyes widened, and he asked, "The FBI agent?"

"That's the one," Stone whispered out of the side of her mouth.

Cross chuckled and said, "Told ya this day was gonna suck."

"Yup, this day just turned to shit real quick," Stone replied.

"Come on in," Reed said.

The three sat at the back two tables while Reed began to speak. "Now that everyone's here. Let's begin. Shall we? Now, as you know, Stone and her new partner, Raylon Cross, have been investigating two recent murders, which have all the hallmarks of a serial killer. That is why we're all here ... in this room. For now, it's stayed out of the news, and nobody outside of a very few people knows these two murders are linked."

After pausing briefly to let the news sink in, Reed continued, "This department does not want another Larry Gene Bell on our hands, so we're getting proactive extremely quickly."

Cross leaned over to Stone and asked, "Who's Larry Gene Bell?"

Stone quietly replied, "A Lexington County serial killer who killed at least four people before being caught and arrested. He was executed in October of 96."

Cross nodded and continued listening to Reed. "For that reason, we have brought in some additional help. Special Agent Peter Davenport of the FBI and my counterparts in the Newberry, Saluda, and, if need be, Richland County Sheriff's Department are all standing by to assist. Everything has already been cleared with their respective departments, and you are free and clear to operate wherever this case may take you. That said, I want to bring Special Agent Davenport up to say a few words."

As Davenport began to speak, he looked around the room, and as his eyes settled on Stone, he gave a nearly imperceptible smile. She, in turn, stared down at the table. Watts noticed what was happening, leaned closer to Cross, and asked, "What's with the vibe between those two?"

Cross chuckled and whispered, "You, my brother, have some competition."

"Great, just great," Watts replied as he tossed a pencil onto the table. "Just when I thought I might have a chance."

"Just to be clear, you never had a chance," Cross whispered, smiling.

"As I was saying," Davenport said to get everyone's attention, "I have sent copies of both QR codes to my people in cybercrimes. They will do their best, but they are not hopeful. These days, QR codes are a dime a dozen and, if done properly, nearly impossible to trace. Many times, serial killers taunt the police when they make contact. This guy is different, though. He seems to want or need to be caught. He almost appears to feel empathy for his victims."

Watts asked, "Why leave them on the islands?"

"That is an excellent question ... Um, what's your name, officer?"

"It's Russell Watts, and it's game warden, actually."

"I see," Davenport replied, "and why are you here?"

"Because I'm just that damn good," Watts replied smartly to the chuckles of the others in the room.

"Actually, he's on loan to us from SCDNR until the matter on the lake is settled," Undersheriff Reed replied. "He is to act as a ... liaison of sorts on all things concerning the lake."

"You mean babysitter," Davenport replied to Reed.

"Not necessarily," Reed retorted, "Watts is highly qualified and one of the best on the lake."

"Only *one* of the best?" Davenport asked.

"Well, I don't mean to toot my own horn, but I am one of the top two or three, I'd say," Watts replied with his usual antagonistic behavior.

Reed stood and said, "At any rate, we need to get a move on and catch this guy before the news gets wind of it and it becomes a circus around here. If anyone needs anything, let me know. Now, get to it."

Davenport walked through the group and directly up to Stone as the meeting broke up. He smiled and said, "It's good to see you again. You look good."

Stone replied, "So do you." Stone immediately turned to Cross and said, "This is Raylon Cross, my new partner."

Cross took a half step closer and extended his hand to shake hands with Davenport. As they shook, Stone could see Davenport's fingers turning red as Cross squeezed.

"You have some grip," Davenport said, trying not to show pain as Cross attempted to squeeze the blood out of Davenport's hand.

"Sorry about that," Cross said as he let go. "Sometimes I don't know my own strength."

"No problem," Davenport replied as he tried to inconspicuously rub his hand after Cross let go. Davenport looked at Stone and said, "Can we talk?"

"Sure, go ahead," Stone said with Cross and Watts standing there. "Talk."

"I mean privately," Davenport replied.

Stone huffed and said, "We can talk across the hall," as she walked toward the door.

Davenport followed her, and as they reached the doorway, Cross said aloud, "If you need anything, just call out. Watts and I will go over developments in the case with Reed."

Stone nodded her head, understanding what Cross was implying.

Stone led Davenport across the hallway to a small storage room, closed the door, and said, "So, talk."

"First of all, it's great to see you. You look good." Davenport said smoothly.

"Save it," Stone replied. "You obviously chose the job over me, so I see how I rate with you. And for you to leave like that!" she blasted, "I've never felt so humiliated. We were doing great one day, and you were just gone the next!"

"Look, you have every right to be pissed. If you remember, I was here on vacation ... an emergency situation arose elsewhere that I was tasked to deal with. I had no choice."

"I know! But you didn't call, email, text, or anything!" Stone snapped. "You just left."

"I didn't know what to say or do," Davenport replied dejectedly. "I was scared."

"Of what?" Stone asked.

Davenport paused and said, "I don't know ... maybe that it was getting too real too fast and that I was going to have to choose between you and the job sooner or later, so when this emergency happened, I took it as a sign."

"Yeah, and you picked the job over me," Stone said as she reached for the door handle to leave.

"I messed up. I know that now, but you have to see it from my perspective. I had to choose between my dream job and my dream woman ... I chose wrong."

"Clearly, you did," Stone said as she let out an ever-so-thin smile.

As quickly as the thin smile appeared, it vanished. Stone snapped back into her cop persona and said, "Anyway, I'm over you and clearly can't go back knowing that you picked the job over me."

"Stop ... as good as it is to clear the air, it's not why I wanted to talk to you."

Stone's sadness over the pain of their breakup turned into anger in a split second, "You smug son of a bitch! You never wanted to talk about us! Did you?"

In an even tone, Davenport replied, "I need to tell you something, and it's not about us. It's about your father."

9

"What about my father?" Stone snapped.

Davenport asked, "Do you remember the night I was shot at the raid on the Harrington home?"

"I remember. Why?"

Davenport hesitated, then looked around cautiously before lowering his voice and saying, "Remember the room we found with the paintings, the gun, and the notebook written in shorthand?"

"I remember everything. Why? What does any of that have to do with my father?" Stone asked.

"I'm getting to that," Davenport replied as he softened his tone, knowing what Stone was about to hear would hurt. "It took some time before the FBI in Quantico could decipher the book with ninety-five percent accuracy. Your father was named in the book."

"What in the hell do you mean my father was named in the book?" Stone snapped.

"Someone wrote in the book that your father was getting too close. It doesn't mention his murder specifically, but the implication is there." Davenport replied.

"What that means is someone set up my father." Stone snapped.

"Not necessarily. All it says is what I told you the book said, nothing more."

"I believe you. That means my father found out too much and had to be eliminated."

"Yes, but—"

"But nothing," Stone interrupted. "This changes everything."

"Not really," Davenport said. "We still have no idea who or why he was targeted."

"No, but when this is over ... I intend to find out," Stone snapped. "I hate to do it, but I gotta go. We have a long day ahead. Cross and I are headed to Newberry to see if we can get information on our last victim. After we get back from there, hopefully, Doctor Singh will know something about the last victim." Stone turned and walked out without speaking to Davenport, who waited a moment and followed her out.

"Everything good?" Cross asked.

Stone walked past without stopping and replied, "Yep, just awesome. Come on, we need to get going. Someone should be at the restaurant by the time we get there."

Seeing the angered look on Stone's face, Watts slapped Cross on the shoulder and said, "She's all yours today."

Cross shot Watts a death stare and replied sternly, "Don't touch me."

Watts asked, "What are you guys going to do today?"

As Cross followed Stone down the hall, he said over his shoulder, "Cop stuff."

Watts stood in the hallway, and as he watched Stone and Cross walk away, he replied, "Okay, I guess I'll just go back to SCDNR and start looking up boats or something."

Neither Stone nor Cross said a word until they got outside to Stone's car. She tossed him the keys and said, "You're driving."

"Not a problem ... where are we going?"

"Get on I-26 and ride for the next twenty-five miles or so. You'll see the Newberry sign."

After finding his way to the interstate, Cross looked over at Stone, staring out the passenger's window and watching the trees go by. "What's on your mind?" Cross asked.

"Nothing," Stone shot back.

"Something's clearly on your mind, and there's no doubt it has something to do with seeing your ex earlier."

"Yeah, it's something he said about our last case. That's all."

"Talk to me," Cross replied.

Stone huffed and filled in Cross on what Davenport had told her about the book and her father's name being in the book.

"Okay then, if your father's name was in the book, who put it there?" Cross asked.

"There's only one person it could be, and I intend on finding out after our little trip to Newberry is over," Stone replied confidently.

"Wherever this leads ... I'm with you," Cross reassured Stone. "Now, you just sit back and relax for a while."

BEFORE LONG, Cross pulled into the parking lot of The Palms Bar and Grill, which was marked by strategically placed palm trees of different sizes. They parked outside the front door and got out of the car, and headed toward the entrance.

Glancing around the exterior of the building, Cross said, "This is not the first restaurant to be in this building. This looks like it used to be a fast-food joint before it became what it is currently."

"I'll go along with that," Stone said. As the pair approached the front door, a waitress was straightening up inside and saw them standing at the door. When the waitress walked over, she said, "I'm sorry, we do not open for another hour."

Stone and Cross reached into their pockets and produced their credentials. Stone replied, "We're not here to eat. We need to speak with someone in charge, please."

Stone and Cross saw the waitress' cheeks turn red with embarrassment as she unlocked the door and said, "I'm sorry about that. I just assumed you were here to eat."

Cross smiled and said, "It's fine. Is there a manager here we could speak with?"

The young waitress replied, "I can do ya one better than that; one of the owners is here. I'm sure she can help."

Cross smiled and said, "Perfect. What is her name?"

"It's Linda. Linda Smith. Have a seat anywhere, and I'll be right back with her," the young waitress replied.

A few minutes later, another woman walked out, extended her hand to the detectives, and said, "I'm Linda Smith. My husband and I own this restaurant. How can I help you?"

Stone and Cross shook hands with Mrs. Smith and stated, "We are detectives from the Lexington County Sheriff's Office, and we are here to follow up on a piece of information. We hope you can help us."

"I don't know, but I'll try. What kind of information?"

Cross produced his phone and said, "I have a picture of a receipt from here a few days ago. There is what appears to be a card number on the receipt. Is there any way you can tell me anything else about it?" Is there a way to figure out whose name was associated with the card?"

"I'm sorry, but no," Smith replied, "receipts don't have anything identifiable. I wish I could be of more help."

"Do you have security cameras?"

"Yes, we do. Why?"

"Would it be possible to see the camera footage from the date and time this receipt was printed?" Stone asked.

"Sure, come on back," Mrs. Smith replied as she led them into a back office.

It took several minutes for Mrs. Smith to pull up the requested video, but eventually, they saw someone familiar on the screen. As they watched, Cross and Stone could see their victim sitting at a table finishing dinner. Afterward, a waitress arrived, picked up the check, and left to process his bill.

After the waitress left, another man approached their victim's table. They chatted for a moment while the unknown male pointed to the parking lot as they were having a conversation. Before the wait-ress returned with the bill, the unknown man left. Then Cross and Stone watched as the waitress returned; the victim paid and quickly left.

"What in the hell did we just see?" Cross asked.

"I have no idea," Stone replied, "but from this camera angle, we can't even see the other person's face."

"Stone looked at Mrs. Smith and said, "Please tell me you have cameras outside."

"There is one, but it has a limited view and doesn't show much of the actual parking lot."

It took another minute or two for Smith to pull up the exterior video camera, which only showed the same two men walking into the parking lot.

Cross asked, "Has a car been left in the parking lot for an extended period?"

"Yes, actually. Nobody seems to know whose black car that is near the road. It has been there for a couple of days. We figured somebody had broken down and would be coming back for it."

"Thank you," Stone replied with a smile. "Please let us have a look before you do anything."

"Sure, let me know if you need anything else," Mrs. Smith replied.

Both Cross and Stone walked outside to the car and looked inside. "Nothing seems wrong. I don't see anything in plain sight that would get us inside," Cross said as Stone walked to the back of the car.

Cross watched and listened while Stone called a number and said, "Yeah, this is Detective Stone. I need you to run a plate for me."

After giving the plate number and waiting on the phone for a moment, Stone wrote a name down on a notebook she had brought with her and said, "Okay, thanks. Now, can you run a DMV search for this same person?" After waiting another moment, Stone said, "Thanks again."

"Well?" Cross asked.

Stone answered, "This car is registered to Oliver West. He's fifty-six years old, so he fits the age for the body we found on Bomb Island, that's for sure." Stone's phone dinged about that time, indicating she had a new email or text.

Stone made a few taps on her phone, then smiled as she turned the phone toward Cross for him to see. "Recognize him?"

"Sure do! That's our dead guy from Bomb Island," Cross replied.

"The next thing we gotta do is get this car out of here," Stone said. "I'll call Boone and get it processed by our crime scene techs and the car impounded and searched. It isn't very likely, but maybe there will be something useful inside. Let's talk to the owner again and get out of here. We need to be getting back to Lexington."

Cross and Stone thanked Mrs. Smith for her help, and Stone left a card for her in case she thought of anything else. Cross then told her that they had placed a call with their boss, and someone would be coming soon to remove the car left in the parking lot.

Stone's cell phone rang on their way back to Lexington from Newberry. She looked at the caller ID, which read "SINGH."

Stone showed Cross who was calling and said, "This should be good." Stone answered and put the phone on speaker, "Dr. Singh, this is Detective Stone. You're on speaker with Detective Cross. What have you found?"

"Well, my preliminary report at the scene was correct. The victim died from two stab wounds between the ribs that would have killed the victim within seconds. I also have a name for you. His fingerprints came back to a—"

"Oliver West," Stone replied, interrupting Singh.

"Correct," Singh replied, "but you may be surprised to know how we got a hit."

"Really now? Do tell," Cross said.

"Yes, it would seem that the gentlemen on my autopsy table used to work for us."

"What?" Stone said, shocked.

"Quite right," Singh replied stoically. "I've done some research, and it appears Mr. West's fingerprints were taken when he worked for the coroner's office years ago."

Stone asked, "Would you happen to know what time frame we're talking about that he worked for the coroner's office?"

Singh replied, "Of course I do. He worked for the coroner's office for four years between 1988 and 1991, which was well before my time here."

"Hmmm, the plot thickens," Stone said aloud.

"How? What are you thinking?" Cross asked.

Ignoring Cross for the moment, Stone asked, "Dr. Singh, do you know in what capacity West worked for the coroner's office?"

"Yes, it would seem Mr. West started as an intern, then achieved a full-time job at the lowest level at the coroner's office. Essentially, he retrieved bodies and cataloged various things unrelated to criminal cases. Why?"

"No reason. Thank you, Dr. Singh. We will be in touch," Stone replied before hanging up.

Once the call ended, Stone said, "Now, back to your question, and the answer is, right now, I don't know. It seems ... familiar somehow, but I'm not sure how."

Cross asked, "Okay, then, if this West character was at the coroner's office before Dr. Singh, who could we talk to about him?"

Stone thought momentarily, and then a smile crept across her face. "I know just the person," she said.

"Who?" Cross asked.

"My old partner, Drew Clayton. At the time of his retirement, he was going at it hot and heavy with the previous coroner, Courtney King, and she had been with the coroner's office for many years. If anyone remembers West, it would be her."

10

Dexter Knoxx walked down the marble steps of his sprawling estate which backed up to Lake Murray, looked at the empty boat slip, and shook his head in despair. He had made his fortune in the late 1980s by running an import/export business with somewhat questionable practices.

In the late 1990s, several agencies, including the DEA and the FBI, started watching his multiple businesses around the Columbia area. Still, by this time, Dexter had mostly retired from his rather lucrative businesses when his only son Connor was born. Not long after, his mother was tragically struck and killed by a drunk driver one night near the family home.

Connor loved the outdoors, having grown up hunting and fishing around the lake. He had always wanted to be a game warden, but he could not attain his dream job because of his father's somewhat checkered past and the stigma of the family name at the time. Instead, fate had another path for Connor.

Against his father's wishes, Connor joined the U.S. Army and entered boot camp at Fort Jackson. Before long, Connor was in Afghanistan assigned to a military police unit. He served with distinction, having been involved in multiple engagements, was wounded in combat, and was awarded the Purple Heart. Eventually, Connor was rotated back to the United States and discharged from the army after being addicted to painkillers after being wounded in Afghanistan.

After his military service, Knox's father, Dexter, sent him to a particular detox facility in California, where he stayed for a time, working to get his life back on track. While there, he bonded with another soldier named Samuel Webb, who had only been at the facility for about a month when Connor left.

Before Connor left the facility, he gave Webb his home information and said he would have a job waiting for him when he was discharged. Nearly a year ago, Webb came to South Carolina to look up his old friend, Connor, and true to his word, Connor got Webb a job as the head of security for a family friend's estate not far away.

However, that is when everything started to spiral out of control for Connor. Unbeknownst to Connor and against his father's warnings, Connor had gotten his friend, Samuel Webb, a job at the home of a monster. Before long, the monster's entire family was being put under a fine-tooth comb until early one morning when the raid happened. When the dust settled, the monster was in jail, and Webb was dead.

Since then, Connor has blamed himself and become more withdrawn from family and friends, preferring to be out on the lake in solitude ... the farthest away he could get from the war in Afghanistan.

Dexter walked to the end of the family's pier, sat on the bench, reached into his blazer pocket, and pulled out a fat Cuban cigar. Reaching into his pants pocket, he pulled out a cigar cutter, clipped one end of the cigar, and stuck it in his mouth. Returning the cigar cutter to its proper place, he again reached into his blazer pocket, pulled out a torch lighter, and lit the cigar. Within moments, Dexter was tasting complex spice, leather, and cocoa flavors as he puffed on the Cuban cigar.

He had been there nearly fifteen minutes, enjoying his cigar in peace and thinking about how best to help his son when the sound of a boat engine caught his ear. As Dexter puffed on his cigar, he watched a bass boat in the lake come closer and closer to his dock.

As the boat approached, it quickly became apparent that his son Connor was returning from an adventure on the lake. Dexter sat and watched as his son expertly pulled the bass boat into the slip, tied it to the dock, and shut the engine off.

Dexter stood and walked over to the boat, picking up a few bags as Connor tossed them from the boat onto the dock. "Hey! Did you have fun?" Dexter asked.

Connor said, "Actually, we did. Usually, being a fishing guide to some city people is quite boring because they don't know how to fish, but this guy was good, and I put him right on some big ones." He had a blast!"

"That's great! That's why you're the best guide on this lake," Dexter replied as he tossed the remnants of his cigar into the lake.

"I don't know about that," Connor replied. "Could you give me a hand getting the gear to the guest house?"

"Sure will," Dexter replied as he grabbed a bag and walked with his son to the guest house where Connor lived.

"You know you can always move into the main house. Right?" Dexter said.

"Yeah, I know, but this way, you get your privacy, and I get mine. That way, if either of us have a girl over, it doesn't get weird."

"I would give anything for you to bring a girl back here," his dad replied, smiling.

"I know, and so would I, but I'm still dealing with ... everything," Connor replied.

"Yeah, I know, son. Anyway, do you have any more clients lined up?"

"I have another one in a couple of days. No biggie, though. It's just another corporate big wig wanting to go on a fishing trip."

"That's okay, though. It's what you love to do, and it pays well," Dexter said. "Not that you have to worry about that, but still, it helps."

"I know, with my military benefits plus what I make as a guide, I have a pretty good life ... most of the time."

As the two walked into the guest house, which was almost as large as a three-car garage, Dexter put his son's bags on the floor, put his hands on his son's shoulders, and said, "The nightmares will go away. It may be a while ... but they will go away."

"How can you be sure?" Connor asked.

"Because mine did, so I know yours will too."

With a puzzled look on his face Connor asked, "What are you talking about?"

"Sit down and let's talk," Dexter said as he motioned for Connor to have a seat. "Not long after high school, I was drafted to go into the army for Vietnam. I did a tour in-country, so I know what you're going through."

"Why haven't you told me any of this before now?" Connor asked.

"For the same reason you don't want to talk about anything. It's still too painful, but the nightmares do go away over time."

"So, what do I do, then?" Connor asked.

"You live your life," Dexter told him, "whatever that is. You know my past ... well, most of it. For me, it was trying to outsmart the cops with my import business. For you, it could be outsmarting the game wardens. You're the best guide on this lake; almost everybody knows it. That's why they come to you. You have to find your passion and dive into it."

Dexter then said, "Well, you've had a long day. Get some rest, and I'll see you soon."

Dexter got up and walked out of the guest house, down the sidewalk, and back to the main house. As he walked in, he poured himself a single malt scotch, plopped down on the couch, and turned on the television to see the local news channel which had a breaking news broadcast.

Dexter sat up and read the banner scrolling across the bottom of the screen, which read:

Body found on Bomb Island in Lake Murray makes two.

∾

As STONE and Cross returned to Lexington, Stone's phone rang. She glanced at the caller's name and said, "It's the boss." As usual, she answered by saying, "This is Stone. I have you on speaker with Cross."

Boone replied, "Well, the cat's out of the bag. Somehow, the media found out about the body on Bomb Island."

"How?" Cross asked.

"Who knows?" Boone exclaimed, "They have a knack of finding out about crap that we don't want to get out. We gotta get a lid on this and quick before something else happens. Tell me you have a plan to figure out who this nutjob is."

"Well, we know who the last victim was; he worked for the coroner's office for a while. According to Dr. Singh, he worked there between eighty-eight and ninety-one. Singh said that was well before his time, but I know someone who may remember him."

"Well, get on it before someone else turns up dead," Boone replied.

"Yes, sir!" Stone replied before hanging up her phone.

Immediately, Stone went through her contacts until she found her old partner, Drew Clayton. Seeing Stone hesitate a moment before pushing the button, Cross asked, "What's wrong?"

"Nothing, just worried that he's out of the game and wouldn't want to get dragged back into something again. That's all," Stone replied.

"Are you serious? He's probably bored out of his mind and looking for something to do."

"I don't know about that. He always said he would be fishing all the time after he retired," Stone replied. "Anyway, here goes nothing."

Stone clicked the speaker button and then hit the button to dial Clayton's number. The phone rang a couple of times, and then suddenly, Stone heard the voice of her old partner saying, "Well, I'll be damned. If it's not my best rookie! How ya doing, kid?"

"Doing good, Drew!" Stone said with a smile. "Listen, I have you on speaker with my new partner, Raylon Cross, and we need to ask a favor."

"New partner! Did you replace me already? Cross, mind your P's and Q's with this one. She's a handful," Clayton said.

"Oh, I already found that out on the first day," Cross replied with a chuckle, thinking about their first meeting in Boone's office.

"So, what can I do for you." Clayton asked.

"Actually, we're after someone else. Are you still seeing Courtney King?"

"Yeah, sure am! Why? What's up?"

"Well, we just caught a case that involves someone who worked at the coroner's office the same time she did. So, she may have known him."

"Well, she's not here right now, but maybe we can meet you two for drinks later tonight. How does that sound?"

"Sounds great!" Stone replied. "I'd love to catch up with you."

"So would I. Besides, I need to check out your new partner to see if he's right for you."

Cross smiled and replied, "I'm sitting right here. I can hear everything you're saying."

Clayton laughed and replied, "Yeah, I know. I'll see you guys tonight at eight."

Before Stone could reply, there was a click as Clayton hung up the phone. "He didn't say where to meet," Cross said.

"There's only one place," Stone said.

The rest of the day was spent at the sheriff's department, making phone calls and tracking leads on Oliver West, the latest victim. After spending most of the afternoon tracking Oliver West, it became apparent that he had decided to move to Newberry after working at the coroner's office.

They also checked in with Special Agent Davenport, who told them the QR codes were a bust as they could have been made in many ways. The website they pointed to was hidden by a VPN, making it look like he could be anywhere from Washington State to Russia.

As it neared five o'clock, Cross asked, "Are you going home to change before meeting your old partner?"

"Nah, I figured I would just stay and work a couple more hours and then leave straight from here," Stone replied, "but you go home and change if you want. I can text you the address."

"You sure you don't mind?" Cross asked.

"Not at all," Stone said.

"Don't forget to text me the address," Cross replied. "I want to meet your ex-partner."

Stone smiled and said, "I'll send it right now, but it's the same place you and I went to the other night for a beer."

"Can't wait," Cross replied.

"I'm not sure if I should be worried or not about you meeting my old partner," Stone said with a smile.

"Oh, yeah, you should be worried. If there are any embarrassing stories, I'm going to find them," Cross said with a chuckle. "I owe you."

Stone laughed and said, "Yeah, ok. Get out of here, and I'll see you there."

LATER THAT NIGHT, Cross pulled into the bar parking lot where the group was supposed to meet. As Cross walked through the parking lot, he saw that Stone was already there. He walked in to find Stone sitting by herself at the bar.

As he approached, he said, "Hey you, your ex-partner and girl-friend haven't shown up yet I see."

As Cross sat down on a stool beside Stone, at the bar she replied, "Not yet. He texted me a few minutes ago, though, and they're on their way."

Cross asked, "So, did you find anything useful after I left?"

"Surprisingly, no. The preliminary reports from Singh show that both of our victims were killed by a knife in the side between the ribs, but other than that, everything else is different."

"I know it's not much, but soldiers are taught to eliminate guards in a very similar manner," Cross replied. It could be that our guy was military."

Stone said, "Yeah, that's a thought, but it doesn't help narrow it down."

At about that time, Cross and Stone heard the door open and turned to see two older individuals walk in. "There they are," Stone said with a smile as she got up and walked over to greet Drew and Courtney.

Cross walked over, standing as tall as he could, and reached out to shake hands with Drew. "You must be her old partner," Cross said as they shook hands.

"That's me ... Drew Clayton," he said as he shook hands with Cross.

"Geeze, you traded up in a huge way. Didn't you?" Clayton said as he smiled at Stone and gave her a friendly hug.

"Yeah, but he's a big teddy bear," Stone said as she looked up at Cross and patted him on the arm.

Cross rolled his eyes and said to Courtney King, "Anyway, my name is Raylon Cross, and we hope you can help us with a case."

"Well, let's get a booth and have a chat. Shall we?" Courtney replied.

The four went back to a booth away from everyone else in the corner of the bar and took a seat. After they sat down, a waitress came to take their order. They all ordered beers and made small talk until the waitress returned with their drinks.

As soon as the waitress left, King asked, "So, Drew says you wanted to talk to me about a case."

"Something like that," Stone replied. "Recently, there have been a couple of murders where the victims have been left out on different islands in Lake Murray. Strangely, one of the victims used to work for the coroner's office at the same time you did."

"My God!" Courtney replied. "What's the name?"

"The victim's name is Oliver West. He supposedly worked there from 1988 to 1991. Did you know him?"

King thought for a moment and said, "I knew of him. I wouldn't say I knew him. From what I remember, his work was not the best, and he was a low-level intern or something of that nature. I don't think he had the attention to detail it took to work for the coroner's office."

"What happened after he left the coroner's office?" Drew asked.

Cross replied, "We're not entirely sure. He moved up to Newberry, where he dropped off the grid. We haven't looked at his financials yet, but I doubt there will be anything worth looking at."

Stone smirked and said, "I wouldn't be too sure about that. I called in a favor and got a look at his financial records after you left a little while ago. It seems Mr. West has made cash deposits ranging from one to five thousand dollars off and on since he left the coroner's office."

"Where does he work?" Cross asked.

"As far as I can tell, he worked several odd jobs here and there, but nothing that would account for the amount of money he's been depositing," Stone said.

"Sounds like a payoff then," Clayton replied.

"Yeah, but for what?" Cross asked.

"Well, there's something else I haven't told you yet," Stone said as she looked at Clayton.

"I kinda figured. What else is going on?"

Stone looked at the table momentarily, took a sip of her beer, and said, "It's about our last case."

"Talk to me. I can't help if I don't know what's going on," Clayton replied.

Stone took a deep breath and said, "The higher-ups are spooked. These murders have all the hallmarks of a serial killer, so someone brought in the FBI."

Before Stone could say anything, Clayton said, "Don't tell me..."

"Yep, someone thought that since Davenport had been here already, bringing him back would be a good idea. Well, remember the night he got shot on the raid at the Harrington Estate?"

"Sure, I remember," Clayton replied.

Stone replied, "So, in the secret room where we found the paintings, we found a desk, and in that desk was a notebook written in a special shorthand."

"Yeah, I remember. Why?" Clayton replied.

Davenport told me that the FBI was finally able to decipher the book with 95% accuracy, and my father's name was in that book."

Clayton's eyes widened, and he said, "Holy shit! How exactly was your father named in the book?"

"All Davenport would say was that the book stated that my father was getting too close to discovering the truth. It does not say he needed to be eliminated, but the implication is that he was too close for comfort."

Courtney held up her hand and said, "Wait a minute, guys, I have a question. Amy, do you mind sharing the details of your father's death?"

Stone took a breath and said, "As the story goes, he was investigating allegations of some rather unusual happenings on Lake Murray. An informant supposedly wanted to meet my father one night with some information, but it was a setup. He supposedly thought a cop was protecting someone on the lake."

"So, he went to meet the informant alone?" Cross asked.

"Yeah, the word was, he was ambushed and shot while he sat in his car. He never knew what hit him. Detectives at the time assumed he knew who had shot him because he was shot at basically point-blank range."

"When was this?" Courtney asked.

"1989," Stone said, taking a deep breath.

Courtney replied, "So, is it me, or does anybody else find it disturbing that all this happened around the same time frame?"

"What are you thinking?" Cross asked.

Instead of answering Cross, Courtney said, "And there's something else, too." Courtney glanced at Clayton and said, "Remember when you two came to me working on that case, and I found that file for Peter Harrington had been forged?"

"Yeah, I remember. Why?"

Courtney stared at Clayton momentarily and said, "Oliver West would have had access to the files back then. He very well could have done it."

"So, what are we saying here?" Cross asked.

"We're saying that there's more here than meets the eye. That's for sure," Stone replied.

"You know what your next step is?" Clayton asked.

"Yep ... we gotta talk to Beatrice Harrington," Stone replied.

11

The same night Stone and Cross were getting together with her ex-partner and his girlfriend, the man again found himself alone, this time on Susie Ebert Island. After setting up camp for the night, the man set up a nice fire. Once the coals were suitable, he cooked himself two hamburgers and ate them silently by the water's edge.

It's so peaceful. The man thought to himself as he listened to the sounds of the lake ... *I wish I could stay here. It's the only time my brain seems free and at rest.*

After sitting by the fire until it died out and watching the twinkle of the small lights onshore, the man yawned, yearning for a peaceful night's sleep. "At least I'm not on Goat Island. I'm never going back there again," the man said aloud, even though he was alone.

Cracking open a beer he had brought with him, the man sat there, clearing his mind and drinking his one beer in complete silence. Finally, after a long yawn, he glanced at his watch to see it was well past eleven o'clock at night. "Well, I guess I need to get some sleep," the man said as he stood up, stretched, and headed into his tent for the night.

Before long, the man was sound asleep. However, it did not last.

In the early morning hours before dawn, something hit the side of his tent, waking him. The man instinctively jerked himself awake and reached for his weapon sitting on the ground beside him.

Listening for another moment or two, he didn't hear anything else, and before long, he was drifting back asleep. Then, as if in a dream, the man found himself standing outside his tent, staring across the lake, mesmerized.

Frozen in place, the man was horrified to see a dark figure with glowing red eyes appear out of the lake. *Not again,* the man thought as he could not move ... frozen in place, just like the last time.

The man watched as the figure slowly approached him, and just like before, all he could see were the eerie red eyes and darkness ... nothing more. Suddenly, the man felt rather than heard. *You've done well, but I require someone more ... experienced, more ... substantial.*

"It will be as you say..." the man muttered.

Bring me ... a police officer.

"And I know just the person for you," the man said.

The next thing the man knew, he was standing in the middle of his camp, overlooking the lake as the sun rose. The man involuntarily shuddered, snapping himself the rest of the way out of his trance-like state.

Glancing around, he quickly began to pack his camp up and return to shore, still unsure of what had just transpired ... yet again.

THE NEXT MORNING, Stone and Cross went straight to Boone's office, knocked on the door, and walked in without waiting, announcing, "We need to talk."

"Well, come right in," Boone said, rather miffed that they would come in without being given permission first. "What's going on?"

"We've been running down a lead, and I don't want to say right now, but it appears there is a link between Beatrice Harrington and this case."

"What ... how?" Boone stuttered.

After filling Boone in on what they had discovered, Boone said, "Wait a moment." They watched as Boone picked up the phone and dialed a number. Momentarily, Boone said, "Come to my office," and then hung up.

A few moments later, there was a knock on Boone's door, and FBI Special Agent Davenport stuck his head in, saying, "You wanted to see me?"

"Yes, come in," Boone said.

Stone rolled her eyes and said, "We can handle this. We don't need his help."

"I know you can handle it," Boone replied, "I just believe that a little extra muscle won't hurt. Beatrice Harrington is currently being held at the Women's Correctional Facility off Broad River Road. I want you three to go have a little chat with her. I'll call ahead and make the notifications."

"What in the hell is going on?" Davenport asked.

"We'll catch you up in the car on the way," Stone replied as the meeting broke up. She pushed past Davenport and said, "Better hurry up."

Davenport looked at Cross and asked, "What did I do?"

Cross held up both hands, smiled, and said, "Hey, I'm new here. I'm not getting in the middle of it, but you better find a way to fix whatever this is."

Davenport glanced at Boone and asked, "Are you sure this is a good idea?"

"Nope, but I'm enjoying watching the show," Boone snickered.

Davenport shook his head, turned, and walked out. As Davenport and Cross caught up with Stone, Davenport inquired, "So, what's going on?"

Without even making eye contact with Davenport, Stone said, "We just recently connected Beatrice Harrington to one of the victims in our current case ... not to mention what you told me about my father's death."

"So, you think it's all connected?" Davenport asked as they walked through the parking lot to Stone's car.

"It's looking like it is," Stone said.

As they reached Stone's car, Davenport walked around to the passenger's side seat and started to get in. When Stone saw what he was doing, she asked sternly, "What do you think you're doing? My partner rides up front with me. You're in the back seat."

Davenport huffed and uttered, "All right, all right."

After a tense and silent ride, the three pulled into the Women's Correctional Facility parking lot and hopped out. After Davenport got out, he said to no one in particular, "That was a fun ride."

"And now the party's really getting started," Stone replied.

The three checked in at the front desk. They had to place their service weapons along with their handcuffs, ammo and knives in secure lock boxes before entering the facility.

Once the three relinquished their weapons, they were escorted to an interview room, where Beatrice Harrington and an attorney waited anxiously.

As soon as they entered the room, Stone noticed that the haggard old lady looked like she had aged a decade, even though it had only been a few months. "Well, well, well," Harrington said as she looked at her visitors. "Thought I'd never see you again."

"And yet, here we are," Stone replied sarcastically as she and Davenport took a seat directly across from her while Cross leaned against the wall.

Harrington looked at Stone and Davenport and replied, "I remember both of you." Then her focus shifted to Cross. "But I don't remember you. What was your name again?"

"You don't need to know my name," Cross snapped.

Davenport redirected the conversation and said, "The FBI managed to decipher your coded book."

An evil smile crept across Harrington's face, and she replied, "Oh, you did. Did you? So, that's why you're here."

Davenport replied, "Yes, that's why we're here. It would seem that someone that used to work for you just turned up dead, and we want to know why."

"How should I know why? I've been locked up in here, and,

except for my attorney, I haven't had a single visitor since my two supposed sons took my money and ran. Who was killed?"

Stone said, "A man named Oliver West. We believe he was on your payroll several years ago. He was living above his means in Newberry, and suddenly, he turned up dead compliments of a knife between the ribs."

Harrington started to reply, but the lawyer touched her arm to stop her. "Wish I could help you, but my memory is not what it used to be."

"What are you offering?" Harrington's lawyer asked.

"What do you want?" Davenport asked.

As cliché as it may have been, Harrington leaned in close and whispered something into her lawyer's ear. Then the lawyer sat up and said, "Time served."

"Hell no!" Stone snapped. "You orchestrated at least one murder and got him shot!" she said as she pointed her finger at Davenport.

"Then I'm sorry, but it's no deal," Harrington sneered.

Davenport started to reply to Harrington, but Stone stopped him and said, "Don't, we'll find another way."

Stone said, "Let's go."

Cross opened the door, and as Stone and Davenport stood and stepped toward the door they heard Harrington say from behind them, "Veritas Aequitas ... Truth and Justice ... your father's killer is still out there and close by."

Stone stopped dead in her tracks momentarily but walked out, slamming the door behind her without even making eye contact with Harrington.

As soon as she heard the door slam shut, Stone exhaled and leaned on the wall, taking a deep breath. "Why did she have to say that?"

"She's trying to get under your skin," Cross replied. "Is there a chance she's right though?"

Stone looked at Cross, shrugged her shoulders, and said, "Yeah, there's always a chance, but I haven't seen anything in any report that leads to the Harringtons other than what Davenport told me."

"But the fact that your father's name was in their coded book, and she just mentioned it in there, lends credence to the fact that she knows something," Davenport replied.

"Yeah, I hear you," Stone replied, "but if we were to make this deal, my father would roll over in his grave ... I just can't do that."

Davenport said, "But—"

Before he could say anything else, Cross stepped closer, interrupting him mid-sentence and saying sternly, "But nothing. She said no."

Davenport snapped, "Okay, whatever ... look, if you don't want to catch your father's killer, it's on you, but the answer is in that room!"

Cross took another half-step closer to Davenport with his imposing frame so their noses were almost touching. He replied calmly, "And we're going to get the answer, but not now. Right now, our focus is who is murdering people and leaving them on the islands in the lake."

Stone replied, "Easy there, big man. It's okay."

Cross took a step back from Davenport, who tried not to show it but was visibly relieved that Cross took a step back and separated the two. The three started walking away from the interview room when they heard the door open behind them. All three turned to see Harrington's lawyer walk out.

"You know what she's doing is wrong. Don't you, counselor?" Davenport said smugly.

The lawyer turned toward Davenport and said, "I know nothing of the sort," then turned and left.

The three then walked toward the front of the facility, where they retrieved their service weapons and returned to Stone's car.

STONE'S PHONE rang on their way back to the sheriff's department. As usual, she looked to see who was calling, put it on speaker, and said, "Hey boss. I have you on speaker with Cross and Davenport. What's up?"

"Tell me you were able to find something out from Harrington," Boone stated.

"Yes and no," Stone replied, "The old witch says she can point me in the direction of my father's killer, but she wants to be released for time served. Of course, I feel like she knows more than what she's saying, but without a deal, she won't say."

"Well ... you three better figure this out ASAP because another QR code has been delivered to the station," Boone replied. "I've already directed the envelope to have copies made and the original to be processed."

"Have you scanned the code yet?" Stone asked.

"Yeah, I have, and you won't believe where it leads to," Boone responded.

"I'm scared to ask, but where?" Stone replied.

"GPS coordinates show Spence Island near Bomb Island," Boone replied.

"We're on our way," Stone said.

"Don't come here. Go straight to the boat ramp where you met Watts before. He'll be waiting for you. I know you don't like him, but since SCDNR knows the lake and all the islands better than any of our people, there's not much of a choice."

Cross said, "Isn't there anybody else? Anybody at all?"

Boone said, "Sorry, but no, he is SCDNR's best on the islands in the lake. And remember, he has been temporarily assigned to us."

"Great, just great," Cross replied.

"You three get going," Boone replied.

After Stone hung up from talking with Boone, Cross snapped, "Whoever this killer is ... he's really starting to piss me off."

12

Not long after hanging up with Boone, Stone parked at the nearest marina. All three got out and almost immediately spotted Watts' boat tied to the end of one of the piers.

As they walked toward the end of the floating pier where Watts and his boat were located, Watts saw them coming, spread his arms wide, and said, "Amigos! My baby's all fixed up and ready to go! Where are we going this time?"

"Spence Island," Stone replied.

"Well, let's get loaded up. Shall we?" Watts replied.

Stone told Watts, "You remember Davenport, don't you?"

"Sure do," Watts replied. So, here's what we're going to do. You and Cross will have to squeeze together on the bench seat in front of the console. Of course, that leaves none other than Stone riding with me. Get situated while I untie the boat and push us off."

All three put on their life jackets and took their seats. Before long, they were speeding across Lake Murray to Spence Island. After the fifteen-minute trip, Watts reduced the boat's throttle as they slowly pulled up to the oddly shaped island.

As they slowly circled the island, Watts said, "There's a small beach along the opposite side of the island. I will swing around there so we can pull right up to shore."

A few minutes later, everyone aboard felt the boat lurch to a sudden stop as the boat's bow hit the sandy beach. All three watched as Watts opened a compartment on the bow and pulled out a large length of rope. He tied one end to a cleat on the bow, then jumped off the boat onto the beach.

"You guys coming, or are you going to stay on the boat?" Watts asked.

"We're coming! I was just wondering what you were doing with the rope," Stone replied.

"Considering what happened the last time, we were out here, I thought I would put us on the beach this time. Now, all I gotta do is tie us off to one of these trees, and we should be good."

"Wait, what happened last time?" Davenport asked.

"You don't want to know," Watts replied, shaking his head. "Not my finest hour."

Once the boat was tied up, Watts said, "Okay, let's move inland. There is nothing on this island but trees and underbrush. It is a bit bigger than the other islands, though, so we might want to consider splitting up to cover more ground faster."

Everyone agreed, then Watts looked at Stone, smiled, and said, "Well, I guess that means you're with me."

"Nope," Cross replied sternly, "She's my partner, I go where she goes."

"Alright, Alright. I'll take Davenport then," Watts said, much to Stone's amusement.

The two teams were separated by fifteen yards, and each duo slowly and methodically worked their way to the coordinates provided by the latest QR code, looking for anything unusual as they went.

Twenty minutes into their search, Cross called out, "I've got a body!"

Everyone converged on the spot where Cross was standing. As they approached, everyone could plainly see there was yet another body just like the last, almost perfectly intact and posed like all the others, but this one was different.

All four looked down on the body of a male who couldn't be any more than twenty or twenty-five years old. "This ... this clearly is not his typical victim," Cross said.

Nobody spoke for a moment, stunned at what they were looking at. Davenport was the next to speak, saying, "He's still a baby."

After a moment, Stone said, "We ... we gotta call this in."

Stone took a few steps away and made the call they all dreaded. Everyone listened as Stone said sadly, "Hey boss ... yeah, we're here at the coordinates, and we have another body. He looks to be a twenty-five-year-old kid at most ... yeah, we'll need everybody again."

After listening to what Boone told her, Stone hung up the phone, looked up, and said, "He was already prepared for this. He had everything on standby and was waiting for confirmation from us. They're already heading this way."

Cross cautiously circled the body and said, "Looks like the manner of death is the same: two stab wounds between the ribs on the right side."

"So, we know the killer must be right-handed, then," Watts said.

"Yeah, but that doesn't help us much," Davenport replied.

Stone looked at Cross and could see the wheels spinning in his head. She asked, "Cross, what is it? You're thinking hard about something. What is it?"

"I don't know, this kid is ... familiar somehow. I just don't know how."

"Have you seen him before?" Stone inquired.

"No, but he is definitely familiar."

"Well, it would seem that we have plenty of time for you to figure it out," Davenport replied as he swatted a mosquito.

"I know I haven't seen him, but somehow he is familiar to me," Cross replied, racking his brain trying to figure out why this kid was so familiar.

After ten minutes of near silence from Cross, his eyes widened. He snapped his fingers and nearly shouted, "I've got it!"

"What is it?" Stone asked while Davenport and Watts looked on.

"Do you remember the old fisherman I talked to on the pier by the boat slip that day?"

"Yeah, I do. Why?" Stone asked.

Cross pointed at the victim and said, "He fits the description the old fisherman gave me to a tee! That's why he seems familiar to me!"

"You gotta have more to go on than that," Davenport replied.

"I know, I know," Cross replied excitedly, but that is why this kid feels familiar to me. There's no doubt."

Stone said, "In that case, we first need to identify this body."

"Exactly," Cross replied.

"I hate to be the bearer of bad news, but many people have brown hair and eyes. It's not that uncommon," Watts replied.

Cross replied, "True, but if we can get a photo of the body and find that old fisherman again ... it's possible he can identify the guy as the one he saw leaving a note on your car."

"It's a long shot, but we don't have anything else to go on," Davenport replied.

"And if we can find the fisherman and he can identify this guy as the one he saw that day, which would mean he had to have been working with the killer," Cross replied. "Why else would he leave a note on your car?"

"Not necessarily," Watts replied. "For all we know ... this note you guys are talking about was left on the wrong car."

"I hate to say it, but he does have a point," Cross replied.

"Yeah, I know, but right now, it's the only thing we have until we identify this guy," Stone said as she looked at the victim.

ONE HOUR LATER, Dr. Singh and several people from the coroner's office arrived with the crime scene unit. "We really have to stop meeting out here like this," Singh said stoically as he walked up to the location of the body.

"I know, right?" Stone said.

"What do we have?" Singh asked.

"Pretty much the same thing as last time. An adult male with what appears to be two stab wounds to the right side and his arms folded across his chest."

After examining the victim for only a moment or two, Singh said, "Of course, I won't know until I get him back to do a full postmortem examination, but this definitely looks like the same guy's work."

While Stone was talking to Dr. Singh, Cross walked over to the crime scene photographer and told him to make sure he got a head and shoulders shot to show in case he was able to find the fisherman.

Two hours later, Stone and Cross found Dr. Singh and his workers preparing the victim for transport. While finishing up, Cross walked over to Singh and asked, "Hey doc, you wouldn't happen to have found a wallet or ID on the body, would you?"

As soon as Cross said it, Stone cringed, knowing what was about to happen.

Singh stopped what he was doing, looked at Cross eye to eye, and said, "I know we haven't worked together that much, and you're fairly new to my crime scenes, but let me say this ... my proper designation is doctor. You may address me as Dr. Singh, or just Singh if you prefer ... but never doc."

"Yes, sir. I will remember that from now on," Cross replied, "but the question still stands. Did you find any identification on the body?"

Singh broke the staring competition first before turning away and said, "No, we did not."

Watts, who had been standing back out of the way watching, spoke up and said, "I have a question."

"What's that?" Stone asked.

"If, and I'm not saying he is, but if that is the same person who left a note on your car the day we were stuck on Bomb Island ... where's the boat?"

Cross looked at Stone, who swatted a mosquito off her arm and said, "That's a good question. Do you have any ideas?"

"Not really," Watts replied. There are literally thousands of boats up here on the lake. Without a registration number, it will be impossible to find."

Stone said, "What is it, Watts?" I can see your wheels turning."

Watts thought momentarily, then responded, "Remember when I said I was one of the best on the lake?"

"Yeah, we remember. Why?" Cross asked.

"Well ... I just may know somebody who can help us. When I say he knows this lake I mean he *knows* this lake. He is without question the best guide around," Watts replied.

"Okay, so who is he?" Cross asked.

"That's the thing he—"

"Here we go," Stone said, interrupting Watts.

"As I was starting to say before I was so rudely interrupted," Watts replied, "his family name is not exactly the best around here."

"Meaning what?" Stone asked.

"He wanted to be a game warden, but ... let's just say that because of his father's name, he couldn't get a job with us ... or any department for that matter. Nobody would touch him."

Just then, Singh walked over to where the three were talking and said, "Okay, we're done here. We're going to transport the victim back to the coroner's office for a full postmortem exam."

As Sing turned to walk off, Cross glanced at Stone, and an ever-so-small smile spread across Cross' face as he replied, "Thanks, Doc."

Dr. Singh paused briefly as if he were going to turn and say something, but he kept going. Stone giggled and said, "Better be careful. He's already sent an email to Boone about me."

Cross shrugged and said, "Oh, well, just poking a little fun at the stuck-up prude. He reminds me of some of the old ladies in my church back home."

Stone laughed and said, "Okay, Watts, back to you. What's this guy's name that you're talking about?"

"Are you sure you want to know? I mean, he does have some experience in investigations. After he found out nobody around here would hire him, he went into the military and became a military police officer."

"Getting better all the time. Keep talking," Stone replied.

"From what I've heard, he stayed in the Middle East for a year or so before being wounded in an attack. Supposedly, he got hooked on painkillers for a while, but after his rich daddy sent him to California to get clean, he came back home where he now thrives on the lake."

"Okay, so what's this guy's name?" Stone asked.

"His name is Connor Knoxx. He lives in a huge mansion on the lake. Actually, from what I've heard, his father lives in the mansion. He lives in the guest house, which is like a normal-sized house."

"And what do you think he can do for us?" Stone asked.

"If there's anything happening on the lake, he's the one to go to. He loves the lake and has helped SCDNR before," Watts replied.

"Well, when we get out of here, the first order of business is to find an ID on this body. Then we will talk to Mr. Knoxx," Stone replied.

"No, the first order of business is to get something to eat," Cross replied. "Then we will figure out who this guy is."

13

As soon as Watts cut the engine after tying up at the same dock they left from, what seemed like days earlier, Cross asked Stone and Davenport, "Is Creekside okay with you? It's not far from the Sheriff's Department, and the food's great."

Before Stone or Davenport could say anything, Watts weaseled himself into the conversation, saying, "Sorry, I can't. I gotta be getting my baby back and refueled."

"That's good because I wasn't talking to you," Cross replied.

"First off, rude," Watts replied. "Besides, you should be thanking me for helping you as much as I have been on this case."

Stone rolled her eyes and said, "Like you really had a choice."

"Well, no, but that's beside the point," Watts said as Stone, Davenport, and Cross hopped over to the dock and started walking toward the parking lot.

"Don't mind me. I'll just be waiting by the phone," Watts said as the three walked away.

As they got into Stone's car, she said, "Ya know, we really should be nicer to him. He's done a lot to help us so far."

"Yeah, I know," Cross replied, "I just don't feel like listening to him right now. He's too high-strung and doesn't know when to be quiet."

Stone said, "Yeah, I know, but you gotta remember, his job is solitary for the most part, so when he gets somebody to talk to ..."

"I know, I know," Cross replied.

Not long afterward, Stone pulled into the Old Mill parking lot in downtown Lexington and parked. The three walked up the sidewalk into the small yet ample waiting area. Kirt happened to be standing at the pass-through window beside the register and waved as they strolled in through the double doors.

All three waved back, and then one of the friendly waitresses took them to a round table in the center of the floor.

All three ordered cheeseburgers with slightly different condiments. After the waitress left, Davenport asked, "So, what do you think about this case?"

"There's something screwy going on here," Cross replied, "Somehow, I don't think it's a serial killer. I know it's strange to say, but I feel it in my bones that it's not."

"He's acting like a serial, that's for sure," Davenport replied. "After we get done here, I want to run everything we know through the VICAP database to see what I can come up with."

"Sounds good," Stone said.

Before long, their meals came, and there was complete silence at the table as each of them began to devour their cheeseburgers. After the three ate and paid their bill, they started walking back to Stone's car when Cross' cell phone rang.

Cross looked at the caller ID to see one word: SINGH.

Giving Cross an evil little smile, Stone said, "Go ahead and take your medicine. You know what it's about. You know you shouldn't have called him Doc again, but you just had to push his button. Didn't you?"

"Yeah, but it was worth it," Cross said, smiling as he picked up the phone and put it on speaker so Stone and Davenport could hear. "Cross here. What can I do for you, Dr. Singh?"

Singh replied, "First of all, don't think that I didn't notice what you said at the crime scene earlier today—"

"Come on, Dr. Singh, I—"

"Do NOT interrupt me," Singh snapped. "Secondly, it would seem that I have made a positive identification on this morning's victim."

"And who might that be?" Cross asked as everyone listened intently to Singh.

"His name is Buddy Morrison. At the time of death, he was twenty-two years old and had a few minor interactions with the local police, some of which included breaking into cars and relatively minor offenses but enough to get him fingerprinted, which is how I was able to make the identification so rapidly."

"Okay, thank you. Is there anything else?"

"Only other than the manner of death was the same as the others, two knife wounds between the ribs which would have incapacitated the victim almost immediately. After that, it would only be a matter of time before the victim expired."

Cross thanked Dr. Singh and ended the call. As soon as Cross slipped his phone into his pocket, Stone said, "We need to get back so we can run background on this kid and see what he's been up to lately."

No sooner had Stone said that than her phone rang. She took one look and said, "It's the boss. This can't be good."

Stone answered her phone, saying, "Hey boss, this is Stone; you're on speaker with Cross and Davenport. What's up?"

"You guys need to drop what you're doing and return to the department ASAP. Somehow, the local news stations have found out about the deaths on the lake, and they are already stating a serial killer may be on the loose."

"Oh, great! We're on the way," Stone said before hanging up the phone.

Not long afterward, the three pulled back up to the sheriff's department to find a variable circus of news vans up and down the road shooting film using the department as a backdrop.

When the three arrived at the sheriff's department, Boone met them at the door and said, "Whatever resources you need, you will have them. This is spinning out of control quickly. You need to solve this."

While all three walked to Stone and Cross' cubicle, Davenport got on his phone, made a call, and said, "Hey. Yeah, it's me. I need you to get me a background on Buddy Morrison and send it to my phone please and thank you."

Stone looked at Davenport and asked, "What are you doing?"

"Helping. Didn't you hear your boss? We need to solve this quickly, and my people are quicker than yours, not to mention the fact that we have better toys than you guys do."

Cross replied, "He's got a point. They do have way cooler toys."

About that time, Davenport's phone dinged. He glanced at his phone, gave an evil smile, and said, "See what I mean about cooler toys. I already have a background on our latest victim. Let's go."

"Go? Where are we going? We just got back?" Cross asked.

Davenport said, "Well, Stone and I will check out Morrison's last known address."

"I don't think I like the sound of this," Cross replied.

"Well then, in that case, you're really not going to like what I'm about to say," Davenport replied with an evil grin.

"Why don't you and—"

"NO!" Cross snapped, realizing where this was leading, "He gives me a headache."

Stone said, "Look, you heard the boss. We have to split up to cover as much ground as we can as quickly as possible."

Davenport continued, "As I started to say, why don't you call Watts? You two can go talk to this Connor Knox person."

"Somehow, I knew you were going to say that," Cross replied, annoyed.

"And that is why you're a detective," Stone said, smiling.

Cross replied, somewhat irritated, "Times like this; I wish I had stayed back in Alabama."

Stone smiled and said, "Come on, it won't be that bad."

"All right, I'll call him," Cross replied as she and Davenport stood to leave, "The question is ... are you going to be okay?"

"She'll be fine," Davenport replied.

Cross replied sternly, "If she's not … when ya'll get back, me and you will have a little chat."

AFTER THIRTY EARSPLITTING minutes into an hour-long ride to the backside of the lake, Cross and Watts turned into a gated driveway at the end of a cul-de-sac. Cross pulled up to the callbox and pressed a green button. Moments later, through the speaker, Cross and Watts heard a woman's voice with a noticeable Spanish accent say, "Knoxx residence, May I help you?"

Cross held his badge and credentials up to a small camera beside the speaker and said, "My name is Raylon Cross. I am a detective with the Lexington County Sheriff's Department. My associate, Game Warden Russell Watts, and I would like to come inside and talk to Connor Knoxx. Would that be possible? Nothing is wrong; we are working on a case and would like Connor's expertise regarding the lake."

After a brief pause, they heard the woman's voice say, "When the gate opens, please pull all the way up to the main house."

The speaker clicked as it turned off, and the gate suddenly opened before them. As Cross slowly drove onto the property, Watts let out a long whistle and said, "Holy shit! Look at this place! If I owned this property, I'd never leave."

"I know what you mean," Cross replied as he looked across the perfectly kept, and immaculate grounds, which overlooked Lake Murray on three sides. The main house was on the back of the property, farthest away from the street, and the guest house was off to one side of the property.

Near the guest house was a dock extending into the lake, probably sixty-five feet or more. Tied up to the dock was the sharpest bass boat either had ever seen. As they parked and exited their car near the front of the main house, a slightly older man walked down the steps with a cigar hanging out of his mouth. "Good afternoon. I'm

Dexter Knoxx. What can I do for the Lexington County Sheriff's Department today?"

As Cross flashed his badge and credentials, he stated, "I'm Detective Raylon Cross, and this is Game Warden Russell Watts. He's assisting us on a department matter."

Dexter smiled and said, "It wouldn't happen to have anything to do with that supposed serial killer leaving bodies on the islands in the lake, now, would it?"

"And how do you know about that?" Cross inquired.

"It's been all over the local news for the past hour or longer," Dexter explained.

"To answer your question, yes. It is about that. Warden Watts tells me that your son is the best when it comes to Lake Murray, and he is known as an expert regarding the lake. We've come to ask for his help. Is he available to speak with us?"

"Come with me, and we will see," Dexter said as he allowed Cross and Watts to enter the guest house. We call it the guest house, but really, it's my son's house. He lives there so he can have his privacy and come and go as he pleases."

"I see," Cross replied. Tell me, Mr. Knoxx, what do you do?"

"I'm retired," Knoxx replied casually, "but when I was in business, I guess you could say, ... I was in the import and exporting business."

The three walked down the sidewalk to the front of the guest house. Dexter glanced toward the end of the pier and said, "Well, his boat's here. That's a good sign," as he knocked on the door.

Moments later, the door opened, and a middle-aged man stood there sporting a short military-style haircut. His hair was brown, and he had deep, dark brown eyes. His skin was tanned a golden bronze from spending so much time on the lake.

Connor stood momentarily staring at Watts before saying, "You're a game warden. You're not a sheriff."

"That's right. I am a game warden," Watts replied. "We need your help."

"Does this have something to do with what's going on out there?" Knoxx asked, motioning towards the lake.

Cross jumped into the conversation by asking, "So, you've heard already?"

"Yeah, it's been on the news," Connor replied.

"Watts here tells me that you are the go-to guy about this lake. We need help which is why we're here. Mind if we come in?" Cross asked.

"Not at all. Come on in. Take a load off," Connor replied.

Connor led Cross and Watts to the living room while his father, Dexter, sat nearby, paying attention to what was being said.

"Look, somebody is doing some pretty deplorable things out on the lake, and we need your help to catch him," Cross said.

Knoxx was momentarily silent, then said, "Look, I was an MP once in the military, but those days are long over. I haven't had anything to do with the police since I was discharged from the military."

"We understand," Cross replied. We want the benefit of your expertise. I understand that you are the absolute best guide on the lake, and we would appreciate any help you could provide us."

"That's right," Watts replied. "As far as I know, you are a legend around here, and if you love this lake as I am sure you do, you will want to help catch whoever is desecrating what you love the most."

"When would you want me to start?" Connor asked.

"Well, it's a little late this afternoon, so how about this? Can you be at the sheriff's department at nine o'clock in the morning?"

"I'll see you then," Connor replied as he and Dexter stood up to show Cross and Watts to the door.

On their walk back to Cross' car, Cross looked at Watts and said, "You love this lake, don't you?"

"Does it show that much?" Watts asked.

As they returned to Cross' car, Cross opened the driver's side door. He looked across the top of the car's roof at Watts and said, "If you repeat this, I will deny it, but you're a pretty good dude."

"Aw, does that mean we're besties now?" Watts asked.

"Why do you always have to make stuff so ... weird? Get in the car!" Cross snapped.

Knoxx and Dexter watched the two leave and gave a friendly wave as Cross and Watts left. Dexter closed the door when they were out of sight and asked, "Are you sure you want to get mixed up in all of this?"

"What choice do I have? Connor replied.

"I know, son. You've been doing so well with your sobriety. I don't want you to backslide, that's all."

"I'm not going to. I've got it all handled," Connor replied, smiling while looking out across the lake.

ON THE OPPOSITE side of the lake, Stone and Davenport pulled into an old, somewhat dilapidated boatyard, hoping to find information on the lake's newest victim.

"This place isn't creepy or anything," Stone said as she looked around at the state of disrepair on several of the boats. While others didn't look like they had touched the water in years.

Slowly making her way to what appeared to be the office in the back, Stone and Davenport got out and cautiously made their way to the door, looking around as they went to ensure nobody surprised them from behind.

Stone opened the office door and saw a haggard looking older man sitting behind a desk that had not been cleaned in years. "Help ya?" the old man asked in a distinct country accent.

"We're here hoping to gather information on who we believe is one of your employees."

"Really, now? And who might that be?" the old man asked.

"Yes, well, I'm Detective Amy Stone with the Lexington County Sheriff's Department, and this is FBI Special Agent Peter Davenport. Who are you?"

"Name's Samuel Whitfield. Now, who ya lookin' for?"

"As she said, we know where he is but need some background information. Do you know if he has any relatives nearby?"

Samuel started to figure out something must be wrong and asked, "Why don't you ask him?"

Davenport looked at Stone, who replied softly, "We can't. I'm afraid he's dead."

"Dead, huh?" the old man replied. "I'm surprised it took this long. Damn fool kid, he was always mixed up in somethin'."

"Do you happen to know where I can find any of his relatives?" Stone asked.

Whitfield scratched the stubble on his chin and thought briefly before saying, "Well, I guess you're lookin' at him. He's my nephew ... promised his daddy I would look after him after he got locked up on burglary and assault charges. His mama ran off several years ago, leaving me to look out for him. How'd it happen?"

"Someone murdered him," Stone replied.

The old man was silent for a few moments, then said, "Wish I could help ya, but he would come and go all hours of the night. No tellin' what he was up to. I told him not to be bringin' trouble around here."

"Do you happen to know where he was living?" Davenport asked.

"Sure do. There's a trailer on the edge of this property. He spent about half the time there. I have no idea where he went or stayed the rest of the time. I do know he was really into camping and loved the outdoors. My guess is he had a camp somewhere in the woods near the lake, but I have no idea where."

Stone asked, "Mind if we have a look inside the trailer where he stayed sometimes?"

"Sure, just know that whatever you find in there is not mine," the old man reminded them. "Just follow the dirt road to the back of the property, and you'll see an old silver trailer... one of those Airstreams. Just don't mess up anything."

"Thank you," Davenport said, "and we'll be careful."

Stone and Davenport walked back to the car and followed the older man's direction until an old, worn-out Airstream travel trailer appeared. "Geeze, will you look at this thing?" Stone muttered, "It doesn't look like it's been moved in a decade."

"Probably not, but it's got electricity," Davenport said, motioning to the one light still on near the back of the trailer.

They exited the car, cautiously approached the trailer, and knocked on the door. Stone waited a few seconds and knocked again, still getting no response. She banged a third time but harder, and still no response.

Stone unholstered her weapon, reached up, and pulled the door open. After opening the door, she waited a moment, listening for the slightest noise indicating someone may be inside. After waiting a few seconds, Stone called out, "Sheriff's Department, I'm coming in."

Pausing momentarily to be safe, she again shouted, "Sheriff's Department," as she bounded up the steps and into the trailer.

Davenport unholstered his weapon and stood guard at the door of the Airstream, listening to Stone move about inside the trailer. "Did you find anything useful?" Davenport asked while keeping his eyes on their surroundings to ensure nobody could sneak up on them.

Moments later, Stone appeared at the door and said, "No, nothing that would be useful. There are a few bills, personal belongings, and something that looks to be a small baggie of marijuana, but nothing that would tell us how he ended up where he did."

Davenport eased up the steps and stuck his head inside. Looking around, Davenport groaned, "What a sad existence."

Stone replied sadly, "Yeah, but we still owe it to him to catch this bastard. Come on, let's head back."

By the time Stone and Davenport returned to the sheriff's department, it was getting late, and most of the bullpen had cleared out. As Stone and Davenport rounded the corner into her and Cross' cubicle, they were surprised to see Cross still sitting at his desk working.

"What are you still doing here?" Stone asked.

"What kind of partner would I be if I didn't wait to see if you found anything useful?" Cross asked.

"What you really mean Is you're checking on her to make sure she's okay," don't you?" Davenport replied smoothly.

"Could be a little bit of that, too," Cross admitted.

"Where's Watts?" Stone asked. "Tell me you didn't throw him off the dam or anything."

Cross smiled and said, "He's fine. He's coming back in the morning. I hate to say it, but he's kinda growing on me a little."

"Well, that's something," Stone said.

"Did you find anything useful?" Cross asked.

"Na," Stone said. "We talked to an old man who turned out to be his uncle. He showed us where the kid lived, but there wasn't much there. What about you guys?"

"We introduced ourselves to Dexter Knoxx, who then walked us over to talk to Connor."

"And?" Stone asked.

"Knoxx will be here at nine in the morning to lend us his expertise on the lake and his thoughts on the lake in general. It seems he loves the lake just as much as Watts does. I hate to admit it, but Watts was impressive talking to Knoxx."

Stone's eyes widened. She grinned evilly and asked, "Did you two have a bro moment?"

"Not funny," Cross replied as he stood up to leave.

"I'll take that as a no," Stone said, smirking.

"See ya in the morning," Cross replied.

"Want to grab a beer or something?" Davenport asked mischievously.

"Thanks, but no. Considering our past, it would not be a good idea." Stone said. "Besides, I'm exhausted and we have a long day tomorrow."

Stone and Davenport walked out together and talked for another moment in the department's secure parking lot before going their separate ways for the night. Stone turned onto Gibson Road and had no sooner crossed over Hendrix Street when a car pulled out a side street with its high beams on and started tailgating her.

Realizing something was off, Stone pulled her service weapon out of its holster and tucked it between her right thigh and seat belt so she could access it instantly if needed. The mystery car followed Stone up Gibson Road to the stoplight at the corner of West Main Street.

Luckily for Stone, the light was green, and she made a right turn without stopping. The mystery car followed Stone with its high beams still on down West Main until she reached Derrick Street, where she turned off and hammered the gas.

Stone was pushed back in her seat as her cruiser nearly leapt off the pavement from the massive infusion of fuel and raced away from West Main Street. As she approached Grey Street, Stone glanced into her rear-view mirror to see the car trying to catch up but it was far behind after being caught off guard by Stone's sudden burst of speed.

Stone turned left onto Grey Street and hammered the gas again to get to Walker Street, where she again turned left, cut her lights off, and ducked into a parking lot. She had no sooner parked when the car following her sped past, desperate to catch up with its quarry. As the car drove past, Stone pulled back out of the parking lot and turned the tables on the pursuing car. The hunter was now being hunted.

Stone pulled back out onto the road and jammed the gas pedal to the floor, desperately trying to catch up to the other vehicle. As Stone closed on the mysterious vehicle, the driver realized the tables had been turned, slammed on the brakes, and turned onto the nearest side street, hammering the gas pedal and accelerating from Stone at a high speed.

Stone was able to match the mystery car turn for turn but could not get close enough to get the license plate before it disappeared. With her quarry gone, Stone pulled over momentarily to collect herself. Then, she went home via an extended route to be on the safe side.

14

The following morning, Stone arrived early and informed Cross and Boone of what had happened the previous night. Cross was none too pleased that she didn't call him for backup, but she smoothed it over with him by bribing him with a cup of coffee.

As nine o'clock approached, Cross and Stone were notified that Knoxx had arrived at the front desk and a deputy would bring him to the conference room shortly, where the briefing would be held.

Undersheriff Reed had directed their immediate superior, Chief Stephen Boone, to use any and all resources needed to ensure this matter came to a close and quickly. Reed was not too keen on a civilian helping in the case, but considering his background in the military police and his knowledge of Lake Murray, he approved it despite the shady background of Connor's father.

While they waited for the deputy to escort Connor Knoxx to the conference room, Reed and Boone stood off to one side near the front. Reed asked quietly, "Are you sure these two can handle the job, or do you want me to assign a couple of more ... experienced detectives to the case now that the news has gotten wind of it?"

Boone didn't hesitate before responding, "No, sir. Stone was trained by my best detective before he retired, and Cross came to us very highly recommended. I have complete confidence in the pair."

Cross, Stone, and Watts were sitting at a table waiting for the meeting to begin when Davenport entered. "Oh, great," Watts said, rolling his eyes.

"Jealous much?" Stone asked without looking at Watts.

"Only when it comes to you," Watts shot back.

Davenport walked over, sat at the table with the others, and said, "Last night, I did a little digging, and you won't believe what I found on the Knoxx family."

All three leaned closer so Davenport didn't have to talk so loudly. Cross asked, "Okay, what is it?"

Glancing around, Davenport replied just above a whisper, "His father is a man by the name of Dexter Knoxx, and it would seem that earlier in life, Dexter was a naughty boy."

"Do tell," Stone replied.

Cross said, "We met him when Watts and I went to talk to Knoxx. He said he was retired from the import and export business."

"And technically speaking, he was right," Davenport replied. "He did have several businesses, one of which was bringing European furniture into the country, but the other was a small business of exotic cars."

"Okay, so that tracks with what he told Watts and me," Cross replied.

"But here's the thing, neither of his businesses was even remotely big enough to get him that place on the lake, much less allow him to retire at such an early age," Davenport replied. The FBI tracked him for a long time but could not find enough evidence to build a case against him."

"So instead, they blacklisted his son, which is why he couldn't become a game warden like he always dreamed of," Watts replied.

"Correct," Davenport replied as a deputy appeared at the door escorting Knoxx.

As soon as the deputy walked in with Knoxx, Undersheriff Reed and Boone introduced themselves to him and thanked him for coming. Reed went to the front and said, "Let's get started. Shall we? We all know why we're here, but at the suggestion of SCDNR, we reached out to Mr. Connor Knoxx, who, I'm told, is the absolute best on the lake. He was in the army and spent time in the desert with a military police unit, so he's not somebody we just grabbed off the street. He will fill you in on some particulars of the lake that you may not know about."

Knoxx waved and said, "Let me start by saying that I know my family name is not highly regarded in the town of Lexington, but let me be absolutely clear. I am not my father." After a brief pause for effect, Knoxx continued, "I have been briefed on what's going on out on the lake, and I want it to be known upfront that I am not a part of the investigation in any way. I am merely here to give you background information on what you may not know about the lake and why your killer may be doing what he's doing. Now, I will give you a little history lesson on the lake. Does anyone know the year the dam was completed?"

Boone replied, "1930."

"Correct. The dam was started in 1927 and was finished three years later. At the time of its completion, it was the world's largest earthen dam. Many of you have heard stories about the graveyards, buildings, and things on the bottom of the lake ... they're all true, and there's even more than that. Somewhere in the neighborhood of eight small communities had to be bought out and relocated to get the ball rolling on the dam."

Connor paused for a moment to let that sink in. Then he continued, "The topography of the region made it perfect for constructing a damn with the Saluda River running basically right through the valley. With that being said, before the white man came to the valley, Indians, specifically the Saluda Indians, lived here for a time before they left and went north. After leaving, another band of Indians came into the region. They stayed a short time before, poof, they picked up and also migrated north."

Undersheriff Reed interrupted before he could continue, saying,

"That's good and all, but what does that have to do with what's going on out on the lake today."

"Hang on, I'm getting to it," Knoxx replied, "After the Indians left in the mid to late 1800s ... that's when the white men came into the valley and started building communities. But then ... people started dying."

"What do you mean dying?" Stone asked.

Knoxx smiled and asked, "Why indeed? By the time of the Civil War, there were a handful of communities in the valley. By the time the 1920s came around and talks of building the dam spread, there were over a dozen cemeteries and well over 2,000 graves in the valley that folks know of." Again, Knoxx paused for a dramatic effect, then said, "With so few small communities, why so many graves?"

"Poor doctors?" Boone asked.

"Possibly, but it didn't happen anywhere else," Knoxx replied.

"What are you getting at?" Davenport asked.

Knoxx replied, "This is what I'm getting at ... The Indians, who were deeply in tune with nature and spirits, picked up and left. Then, the white men moved in and started dying at much higher rates. Could it be that the Indians knew something the white man didn't?"

Davenport giggled, rolled his eyes, and said, "Are you talking about some voodoo evil spirits or something? Because if you are, I'm not buying it."

"Well, I'm not sure I do either, but people die every single year on the lake, some for no apparent reason, not to mention there are tales of people being hit, touched, and sometimes pulled underwater by some unseen ... force if you will."

Watts spoke up in Knoxx's defense, saying, "I have been to near drowning stories where a survivor has said they felt as if something was pulling them down, so he's not wrong."

"Look, I mean no disrespect, but I still don't get your point," Davenport replied.

"My point is this," Knoxx said emotionless, "If your suspect is killing people and putting them on the islands on the lake like it's being reported in the news and as I've been told, this may be why your killer is doing what he's doing."

"How do you even know it's a male?" Davenport asked.

"Well, the fact that female serial killers are extremely rare for one thing. A female serial killer who can handle a boat, get a body onto a boat, and then drag it onto the island where they are being found is unheard of. I would bet my life on it that it's a man."

Davenport momentarily looked down at the table and then asked, "So, what would you suggest?"

"Well, for starters, I would round up every single DNR and Lexington County boat you can muster, and starting at sundown, I would stop every single boat on the lake I come across, making sure to record the registration number of every single boat. Outfit the boats with night vision goggles if you have to."

Undersheriff Reed said, "I'll call my counterpart over at DNR and see if we can make that happen. Anything else?"

Knoxx replied, "Normally, I would say to patrol marinas and boat landings, but I wouldn't think that would be a good use of resources. If your guy lives on the water or has access to a boat, he may not need a boat landing or marina."

"Agreed," Watts replied, "if we're going to catch him ... it's going to be out on the lake or on one of the islands dumping his next victim. He's too smart to get caught at a boat ramp."

Undersheriff Reed said, "If no one has anything else to add, let's get a move on."

"I'll start making calls and getting things set up," Boone replied as the meeting started to break up.

FOR THE NEXT TWO DAYS, everyone on the team worked every lead they had during the day and helped the Lexington County Sheriff's Marine unit and SCDNR scour the lake at night. They stopped every boat they found, hoping to catch the killer in the act. Cross came up with a rather unconventional solution to the manpower shortage they faced. He pitched the solution to Stone, who was game, so they both went to Boone.

Cross' solution was simple; one of them would be with the boats on the lake at night while the other would work the case as usual during the day. With time not on their side, Boone reluctantly agreed to the idea. Since Stone was a night owl, and she knew Cross wasn't fond of being out on the boats during the day and would hate it at night, Stone volunteered to take the first few nights on the lake.

On the third night, just when the tactic seemed useless, everything seemed to change. Stone and Watts were out patrolling near Goat Island when they heard a call from another SCDNR boat saying they were near Bomb Island and chasing a boat that was refusing to stop.

Immediately, Watts jumped on the radio and said they were coming. Within moments, Stone's shift went from dull, quiet, and boring to a heart-pumping adrenaline rush as coordinates were relayed to Watts. He said, "Hang on!" and jammed the throttle as far forward as possible. In less than a minute, Stone went from half asleep and listening to the gentle hum of the boat to wide awake and hanging on for dear life as Watts rocketed across the water in near darkness.

As they sped across the lake, and even though Stone and Watts were literally shoulder to shoulder, Stone had to shout over the engine's roar and wind, "What would happen if there's a boat out here with no running lights on?"

Watts tried to dodge the question by shouting, "That's against the law. You can't be out at night if you don't have running lights."

"Yeah, but that wasn't the question," she said into his ear.

Watts replied, "At the speed we're going, by the time we saw it, it would be too late to do anything, and let's just leave it at that."

For the next few minutes, Stone kept her eyes peeled as she kept a white-knuckled death grip on the center console while they raced across the massive expanse of Lake Murray in near-total darkness. As Watts and Stone neared Bomb Island, he could see a DNR boat with its lights flashing at high speed. He could not see the boat the DNR boat was chasing, but he could definitely tell that he and Stone were on an intercept course.

Stone listened as Watts picked up the radio and called the pursuing boat, "This is Watts; I am coming in your direction off your starboard bow. How far behind the target boat are you?"

Stone strained her ears, and finally, over the sound of the rushing wind, she heard, "About two hundred yards! He's blacked out and refusing to stop!"

"We're almost there! Stay on him!" Watts called out as he reached up and shut off his blue lights.

"What in the hell are you doing?" Stone asked wild-eyed.

"He doesn't know we're coming. I will sneak up on him before I hit the lights."

"Isn't that a little on the dangerous side?" Stone asked, even though she already knew the answer.

Watts smiled and said, "That's why they pay me the big bucks!"

Suddenly, Stone saw the silhouette of a boat screaming across the lake with the DNR boat hot on his heels. She pointed just off the bow and yelled, "There he is!"

Watts yelled, "Hang on! This is going to be close!"

Stone reached up and held on to the console with everything she had, watching helplessly as Watts rapidly closed in on the still blacked-out boat, trying to evade the other DNR boat.

At less than thirty yards, and while the driver of the blacked-out boat's attention was focused on the pursuing DNR boat, Watts again hit his blue lights, effectively coming out of nowhere.

The pilot of the blacked-out boat panicked and turned hard away from Watts and Stone's boat, but the speed was too great, and the speeding boat nearly flipped over, forcing him to cut his throttle way back to regain control. That was all the time Watts and the chasing DNR boat needed to close in on the fleeing boat from two sides.

In an instant, the pilot of the fleeing boat knew there was nothing else he could do, so he cut his engine and gave up. Stone drew her weapon, jumped aboard, and handcuffed the only occupant of the boat. Once he was secured, Stone yelled, "What in the hell are you doing? Trying to get us all killed?"

The man looked down at the bottom of the boat in despair. Watts and the second DNR boat tied up to the now-stopped boat and flooded it with lights. It quickly became apparent that this man was not the serial killer they had been looking for but rather a fisherman who had been illegally fishing using a freshwater version of fish traps, as indicated by the copious amounts of game fish in the boat and nothing else.

Once they thoroughly searched the man's boat, Stone looked at Watts and said, disheartened, "He obviously isn't the guy we're after, but maybe ... just maybe, he's seen something."

"You don't really think he's going to say? Do you?" Watts asked.

"No, but it's worth a shot," Stone said before nudging the man's foot with hers and asking, "Have you seen anything while you've been out here?"

"What's it worth to ya?" the man asked with a deeply southern drawl.

Stone snapped, "I'm sure Game Warden Watts here would agree that you have a literal boatload of violations here, so we won't take you to jail. That's what you get. Now, start talking."

The man thought for a minute, then said, "Okay, I'll tell ya. I ain't seen nuthin' tonight, but a few nights ago, I seen a feller in a white boat and no runnin' lights haulin' ass away from Bomb Island."

Stone asked, "Did you get close enough to get a registration number or anything?"

"Naw, but I did notice one thing," the man replied in his woodsy accent.

"And what would that be?" Watts snapped.

"The boat had a piece of plywood across the bow like maybe it was set up for duck huntin' or something."

"And that's all you saw?" Stone asked.

"Yep, that's all," the good old country boy replied.

Stone looked at Watts and gave him a nearly imperceptible nod and said, "Okay, Watts, he's all yours."

Watts smiled and said, "I was hoping you would say that!"

Watts looked at the other game warden who initiated the chase and asked, "Are you okay with taking him in?"

"Sure am," he replied.

"Wait a minute!" the man protested. "I thought you said you weren't going to do anything to me?"

"We're not, but we didn't initiate the chase. He did," Stone said as she pointed at the other game warden.

"Oh, come on!" the man said. "I told you what I knew!"

"And the great state of South Carolina thanks you for coming forward, but that still doesn't excuse what you've done," Watts interjected.

The man again started to protest, "But!"

"But nothing!" Watts snapped. "You got us out here chasing you in the dark when we have other matters to attend to! It's gonna take us a while to get you and your boat taken care of and back out there! Besides, you sound like you grew up around here. If you did, you should know better!"

"I know, I know," the man replied disheartened.

It took Watts and the other game warden a little time to get the poacher's boat rigged for towing, and another thirty minutes to tow it to where they could secure the evidence from the boat.

When they finished with the poacher, Watts said, "It will be sunrise in a little while. Do ya want to call it a night?"

Stone thought for a moment, sighed, and said, "Yeah, by the time you take me back to my car, the sun will be coming up. Besides, I'm exhausted. After tonight, I'm ready to do nothing but crawl into bed and sleep."

Watts smiled, saying, "Look at it like this; you will end your shift with a bang. The sunrises over the lake are stunning."

"Well, that's something, I guess," Stone said as they returned to the boat ramp where Stone's car was parked. On the way back to the boat ramp, it slowly became brighter as the sun rose. Neither one spoke, both lost in the moment of the glorious sunrise.

By the time Watts had gotten Stone to within sight of the boat ramp, the sun was up, and they could see people beginning to file into the boat ramp for a day of fun on the lake. As Watts slowed the boat and gently pulled up to a floating dock, Stone spoke for the first time in twenty minutes, saying, "Wow! I hate to say it, but you were right. That sunrise was magical. It made a great ending to an otherwise crappy night."

As Stone hopped out of the boat and onto the floating dock, Watts asked, "So, if this doesn't work, what do we do?"

Stone replied, "We keep working on the evidence. It's sad to say, but we may not find him before he finds his next target."

"And yet another reason in my long list of reasons why I chose to be a game warden instead of a cop," Watts replied. "Go home and go to bed."

"Well, I gotta go to the station first and fill out my nightly log, but then, I will head home for some much-needed sleep. You should go home too. You've been up just as long as I have," Stone said.

Watts let out a long, drawn-out yawn and said, "Believe me, I am."

Stone hopped into her car and drove to the sheriff's department to write her report, which only took her thirty minutes. As she walked out to her car, she bumped into Cross, who was coming in to start his day. "Did you see anything?" Cross asked.

Stone relayed their harrowing chase across the lake in the pitch darkness.

"Well, you go home and go to bed. I'll call you if something important comes up," Cross replied.

"You better," Stone said through half-closed eyes.

"I will, but only if it's important," Cross reaffirmed.

Stone yawned and said, "I'm going home and going to bed now," as she patted him on the arm and started for her car. "Good night. Call me if something changes."

15

Stone went home, took a long hot shower, grabbed a bite to eat, and climbed into bed. She'd had a long and somewhat eventful night, and all she wanted to do was turn her thermostat down low, get under the covers and crash.

Usually, during the summer, she would just let her hair dry naturally, then get up and hit it with a shot of dry shampoo, if necessary, but this time, she took a little extra time to blow-dry her hair before crawling into bed.

As she lay down in the bed, Amy ran her fingers through her hair as she did sometimes, which seemed to help her relax. The last thing she remembered before falling asleep was thinking, *I love the smell of this shampoo.*

Stone was suddenly jolted awake by the BAM, BAM, BAM of someone banging on her door. "Shit!" Stone snapped. "And I was sleeping so good."

Stone jumped out of bed and headed to answer the door. As she walked into her living room, she paused a moment, thinking about the car that had followed her the other night, and then returned to her room to get her gun.

Stone put her hand on the safe's palm reader, and her gun-safe door opened with a click. Stone grabbed her off-duty weapon, checked to ensure a round was chambered, and walked to the door.

Looking through the peephole, she recognized Cross' massive frame standing outside. Relaxing, Stone opened the door, yawned, and asked, "What time is it? I feel like I just laid down."

As Stone let Cross inside, she turned to return her weapon to the safe. As she walked off, he saw what she was holding, and before Cross even realized how it sounded, he said, "Nice piece."

Stone, always sharp and never one to miss a chance to embarrass someone, said, "Thanks. I have a nice gun, too."

"Um, wait! That's not what I meant. I meant ... I meant your weapon. It ... it's a nice gun. What is it a Smith and Wesson?" Cross asked nervously.

Stone walked back into the living room giggling and said, "Relax, I know what you meant, and yes, it's a Smith and Wesson."

Cross took a slow breath and said, "You gotta stop doing that to me. Half the time, I don't know if you're serious or joking."

Stone giggled, and as she walked into the kitchen to fix a cup of coffee, she said, "And again, now you know the real reason why my old partner retired. So, what's going on? What time is it anyway?"

Cross replied, "It's four o'clock, by the way, and you must have really been out cold because I've tried to call several times and could not get you to answer. I was getting worried, so I thought I would come over and check on you."

"What's going on?" Stone asked.

Cross paused for a moment and said, "We have another body, and this time it's a cop."

Stone stopped dead in her tracks, turned, and asked, "What? Who? How?"

Cross replied, "Yeah, this time he called the station and left a message for us that we had a present on Pine Island."

"Who? Who is it?" Stone snapped.

"It's nobody I know. It's a property clerk who used to be a detective. His name is—"

"Jack O'Neal," Stone replied.

"You knew him?" Cross asked.

"I've met him one time. What happened?" Stone asked sadly.

Cross replied, "We've been working the scene for a couple of hours. Singh said it looks like the same guy. Two knife wounds to the right side. The only thing that's different about the crime scene is, technically, we didn't have to take a boat to get there and how the body was found."

Stone thought momentarily and said, "No, but the killer probably did. Even though it's technically an island, Pine Island is, for the most part, accessible by road. There's a small land bridge and a guard shack to keep people off the island who don't belong there."

"Who owns it?" Cross asked as Stone went into her bedroom to change.

"It was owned by the electric company and ran as a retreat for its employees until recently when it was sold to the state. Last I heard, it's still off-limits to the public for now, but it will be a park or something of that nature." As Stone returned to the living room, she said, "Wait a minute. You said something about the way the body was found?"

"Yeah, so, on one end of the island, there is a point that juts out into the lake, and on this point, there is a swing. O'Neal was found sitting upright on that swing as if looking out at the lake."

"Who found him?" Stone asked.

"Some workers found him when they went to do some maintenance. They knew he wasn't supposed to be there, so they went to talk to him, and that's when they realized he was dead."

Stone plopped down on her couch to put on her shoes, and as she did, she asked, "Is there any need to go to the crime scene at this point?"

"No, first responders were called there about eight-thirty this morning. They're undoubtedly wrapping it up if they haven't already by now."

Stone said, "This makes zero sense to me at all, but one thing is for certain, we need to stop by Clayton's place. I need to tell him about O'Neal before he finds out about it on the news."

"Lead the way," Cross replied.

As Stone gave Cross directions on how to get to Clayton's home, she took out her phone and started dialing. "What are you doing?" Cross asked.

"I'm calling Clayton to make sure he's going to be there and tell him not to leave," Stone said as she instinctively put the call on speaker.

After a few rings, they both heard, "Hiya, partner! What's going on?"

"Gotta tell you something. Are you at home?" Stone asked.

"Sure am. As far as I know, Courtney and I will be here the rest of the day." Clayton replied.

"Good. Cross and I are on our way. Don't go anywhere. We need to talk."

"What about? What's going on?" Clayton asked, slightly worried.

"Do you still have your piece?" Stone asked.

"Of course. Why?" Clayton replied.

"Get it out, and if you go anywhere ... go strapped. Cross and I are ten minutes out. I'll fill you in then."

Stone and Cross heard an electric beep through the phone, then a hefty metallic clicking sound as Clayton took his gun out of the gun safe. "See ya in a few minutes," Clayton said with a click.

After a few more turns, Stone and Cross pulled into the driveway of a well-kept split-level home in the back of a quiet neighborhood.

"Nice place," Cross said as he admired the yard's aesthetics.

Smiling, Stone said, "Wait until you see the inside."

As they got out of the car and walked up the sidewalk, the front door opened before they entered the porch. Standing just inside the door, they saw Clayton with his trusty Sig Sauer P365 sticking out of an appendix holster.

Pointing at the weapon, Stone said, "Glad to see you took my warning to heart."

Closing the door and setting his alarm system as she and Cross entered, Clayton replied, "Sure did. What's going on?"

Before Stone could answer, they both heard Cross muttering, "Holy crap! Look at this place." Everywhere Cross looked, he could see all kinds of antiques Clayton had collected over the years. Now, with the antiques that Courtney brought when they moved in together, they had a proverbial museum of artifacts and antiques.

Stone smiled and said, "I told you."

"This place looks like a freakin' museum," Cross said as he let out a long whistle.

Just then, Courtney King, Claytons girlfriend and retired Lexington County Coroner, walked in smiling and said, "You should see the rest of the place."

"Maybe some other time," Cross replied.

As they all had a seat, Clayton asked, "So, what's going on?"

Stone paused and said, "Look, I'm just going to come out and say it. Do you remember on our last case, we went across town to the old property room, and you introduced me to a man named Jack O'Neal?"

Clayton smiled and said, "Sure, I do. Jack and I go way back."

"Well, I'm sorry to say he's dead," Stone said softly.

The news hit Clayton like a runaway locomotive, "What? What happened?" he muttered, shocked, as Courtney put her arm on his shoulder reassuringly.

"As far as we can tell, he was a victim of this killer we've been chasing. He was killed in the same manner as the others. Two stab wounds between the right ribs."

Clayton was stunned at the news that one of his oldest friends was dead, killed by a supposed serial killer. "I ... I find it hard to believe," Clayton muttered, "He was the sharpest detective I knew."

Stone replied softly, "Yes, but from what you told me, he hadn't been on the streets in a long time. You know just as well as I do that your senses dull over time."

Courtney said softly, "At his age, he would have died very quickly."

Clayton paused for a moment, simply staring down at his lap. Then, he looked at Stone and said, "What do you know?"

Stone said, "He was found sitting in a swing on the tip of Pine Island. He had been propped up as if looking out across the lake."

"That makes no sense," Clayton said, "I ... I just can't believe it."

Courtney asked, "Is there a possibility that this is all connected somehow?"

"I'm not sure yet, but it's strange, to say the least," Stone replied. As an awkward silence came over the room, Stone asked, "Drew, I haven't seen the case file in a while, but didn't O'Neal work on my father's case?"

Thinking for a moment, Clayton replied, "Seems like he did. As a matter of fact, I believe he was one of the first detectives to get there. As I recall, he helped to secure the scene and waited for more experienced detectives and the brass to get there. Why?"

Cross asked, "Wait ... Why would the brass have been there?"

"I don't know," Clayton replied, "I do remember it was kept quiet though. As I recall, I heard bits and pieces about your dad being on the trail of something big happening on the lake, but he was tight-lipped about it. I often wondered if he found out who his white whale was."

"What white whale?" Stone asked.

"It was from Moby Dick," Clayton replied.

"I get that, but who was it?" Stone asked impatiently.

With a huff, Clayton said, "I talked to your father not long before he died, and he told me off the record that he suspected a cop of being in on what was happening on the lake, but he never said who. I often wonder if this white whale, whoever he was, killed your dad because he was getting too close to the truth."

Stone stood quickly and practically yelled, "Why haven't you told me this before? Why am I just now finding this out?"

Clayton took a deep breath and replied, "Because I was protecting you. Why do you think I asked you to be assigned to me?"

"What?" Stone asked, shocked.

"That's right. I wanted to ensure you had all the tools you needed when the time came. I just never expected everything to work out like it did. That's all."

"What in the hell are you talking about?" Stone asked, getting more upset by the moment that her partner had kept something from her about her father's death.

Clayton replied, "Look, I kept an eye on you as best as possible while you were on patrol. When you made detective, I quietly pitched it to Boone that we should be paired up together to train you because I knew this day would come. I knew you would find out about your dad eventually, and you would go looking."

Cross said, "So, wait ... let me get this straight. You think her dad was on to something involving smuggling on the lake and another cop was involved. Is that what I'm hearing?"

"Correct," Clayton replied.

"And it's *believed* that her father was meeting someone who had information on what was happening on the lake. Instead, it was a setup, and somebody he knew, likely another cop, killed him to cover up what was going on out on Lake Murray."

"Also correct," Clayton replied.

"But what does that have to do with the killings on the lake going on now?" Cross asked, "And what does that old Harrington bat have to do with everything, or the very first victim for that matter? He was an investment banker from Charlotte. He wasn't even from around here."

"That's a good point." Stone replied, "What did he have to do with anything?"

"I don't know, but I fully intend to find out," Stone said as she shot a not-so-nice look at Clayton. "And I'll talk to you later. Let's go, Cross," Stone snapped as she approached the front door.

"Wait!" Clayton snapped. "What was that about the first victim?"

Cross replied, "He was some sort of investment banker from Charlotte. He was here on a fishing trip. Why?"

"It can't be. It just can't be," Clayton muttered.

"What is it?" Courtney asked, trying to coax it out of him.

"What was the name of the place where your first victim worked?" Clayton asked.

"I don't remember right off hand," Cross replied. "Why?"

"Because—"

"The Pearl Group," Stone snapped from across the room. "Why does that matter?"

Clayton stared at Stone, saying, "Because O'Neal always talked about how good his investment firm was and how I should start using them."

Stone's eyes widened as she made the connection, finally saying, "Don't tell me."

"Yep, The Pearl Group," Clayton replied flatly.

"Do you think he was trying to recruit you?" Cross asked.

"Before, I would have said no, never ... but now, I'm not so sure," Clayton replied.

The room was eerily silent momentarily as everyone seemed to think about what was being said and the implications. Finally, Cross was the brave one who spoke up and asked, "Could this O'Neal guy have been the one that—"

"Murdered my father," Stone finished.

"That doesn't make sense," Clayton replied, trying to defend his old friend. "Why? Why would he do it?"

"Money," Stone replied. "I'll bet he was my father's white whale, and my father got too close. O'Neal would have had no choice but to silence my father."

Clayton stood up and started toward Stone, saying, "Kid, I'm so sorry! I had no idea."

Immediately, Stone put her hands up in a defensive manner, saying, "Don't touch me!"

"I'm sorry, kid! I had no idea. If I had known I would have said something," Clayton replied.

"You should have known!" Stone snapped.

"Everybody, hold on a minute," Cross said calmly. "Everybody settle down. If what we just figured out is true, and that's a huge if ... what does that have to do with the killings going on today?"

Stone replied, glaring at Clayton, "I don't know, but I fully intend to find out! And if I find one shred of evidence, one piece that even leads me to believe that you knew anything ... I'm coming back here, and I will slap the cuffs on you myself."

Stone opened the front door and said, "Let's go Cross. We have work to do."

Cross walked out first, and as Stone turned to leave, they both heard, "Wait, kid, come back. We need to—"

That was the last thing Stone heard as she slammed the front door and stomped back to their car.

16

By the time Stone and Cross got back in the car, tears were streaming down Stone's face—not from sadness but from anger. "You okay?" Cross asked although he already knew the answer.

Without answering his question directly, Stone replied, "Ex-partner or not, I swear, if I find out that he knew anything, I'm coming back here, and I will take extreme pleasure in slapping the cuffs on him. Then, when he goes to prison, I will go there and tell the inmates he's a cop that got busted for child molestation!"

"Whoa there! Slow down a little bit and take a breath. We're getting ahead of ourselves," Cross replied calmly, trying to hide his amusement at how Stone was talking.

"Slow down hell! We're on a roll!" Stone snapped. "Don't you get it? If what Clayton says turns out to be true, there's something bigger going on here, and that would mean it's NOT a serial killer! It would mean every person who has been killed was killed for a specific reason. We gotta look at every single shred of evidence again!"

Before Cross could say anything else, Stone picked up her phone and started dialing. "Who are you calling?" Cross asked.

Stone snapped, "Davenport, I want him to meet us back at the department. I also need him to call Watts and ask him to meet us there. We need to go over every single piece of evidence again from the beginning."

Forty-five minutes later, Davenport joined Stone and Cross back at the sheriff's department, and they gathered in the conference room as they had done previously. They were waiting for Boone to finish a conference call so they could fill him in on what they had discovered. While they waited, Cross asked, "Is Watts going to meet us here?"

Stone grinned and asked, "Why? Do you miss your new friend?"

Cross rolled his eyes and said, "Oh, please. Merely curious, that's all."

Stone giggled and said, "He'll be here. He was out on the lake and said it would take him a while to get here."

About that time, Boone walked in and said, "Okay, so what's this about?"

Stone said, "We're working on a theory, but you aren't going to believe it."

"Oh, really?" Boone said. "Call me intrigued. Start from the beginning."

Stone said, "To do that, we have to start with my father's murder."

"Your father's murder?" Boone asked. "That was 1989. What does that have to do with what's happening now?"

Stone and Cross recounted the conversation they had with Clayton and what Clayton had said about Stone's father investigating something that had been happening out on the lake at the time of his murder.

At that moment, from the doorway, they heard, "What's happening, amigos? Did you miss me?"

Without missing a beat, Stone replied, grinning, "Cross sure did."

"Did not!" Cross replied sharply to everyone's chuckles.

"So, what's going on?" Watts asked.

Stone replied, "For the first time since this all started, we finally have a solid theory, and it's not what we initially thought. At first, we believed it was the work of a serial killer. Now, it looks much more calculated, and someone only wanted us to think it was a serial killer."

"Again, this is reason one hundred and one why I became a game warden instead of a cop," Watts replied. "What do you need?"

Stone asked, "Watts, is there any way you can obtain files on every suspicious death on the lake since 1989?

He thought momentarily and replied, "I'll have to get permission from my bosses, but yeah, it shouldn't be a problem. Can't you do it here, though?"

Boone replied, "We could, but we would have to sift through all the files from Lexington County. What we need are deaths specific to the lake, and we need them in a hurry. So can you do it?"

"No problem. I'll call ya when I'm on the way back," Watts replied

"Thanks," Stone said as Watts headed out.

"What else?" Boone asked.

"Cross and I are going to see Beatrice Harrington again. Most likely, since she only has a public defender and not one of her fancy lawyers, she doesn't know that Jack O'Neal is dead. Maybe we can trip her up into saying something useful."

"What do you want me to do?" Davenport asked.

"What I want you to do is stay here and do a deep dive into every victim that our killer has murdered since this all started. There has to be something there we're missing. I want to know everything about their life from the time they turned sixteen to the time they were killed."

"That's the great thing about the FBI," Davenport replied with a wink. "We're scary good at compiling information. Who do you want me to start with?"

"Start with the first victim that we know of, Jeramy Donahue, then keep going. There has to be something there between all of them. If not, we're screwed."

"Gotcha," Davenport replied.

"What do you need from me?" Boone asked.

"I want to know everything there is to know about Jack O'Neal's record as a cop, starting five years before my father's murder and going until the day he died. Then, I need you to see if you can locate his financial records. If there's something there ... I wanna know it."

"If there's something there, I'll find it," Boone boasted confidently.

"One more thing, chief," Stone said. "We don't know who, if anybody, is involved, so let's keep this as quiet as possible and keep this room off limits for the time being."

"Done," Boone replied. "Now, what else?"

"I think that's it for now," Stone replied.

"Well, get going then, and call me if you need anything," Boone shot back.

"We will," Cross said as the meeting broke up, and they headed for the door.

Boone stopped Cross at the door, nodded toward Stone, and said, "Keep an eye on her. Don't let her do anything ... rash."

"Rash?" Stone asked. "Why do you think I would do anything rash?" Stone reiterated with an evil little smile.

"That evil smile is the reason," Boone replied.

Cross chuckled and said, "I'll keep an eye on her, boss. I promise."

"You better because I'm going to hold you responsible if she does anything stupid."

"Copy that, boss," Cross replied as they walked out.

ONE HOUR LATER, Stone and Cross entered the interrogation room at the Women's Correctional Center where Beatrice Harrington was housed. "Well, well, well, I didn't expect to see you again so soon. Did you come back to make me an offer?" Harrington asked as she looked over at her court-appointed lawyer.

Stone replied, "We came to tell you something and *possibly* make a deal."

"What kind of deal?"

"We would have to settle it with the DA, but we could knock a substantial amount of time off your sentence if and only if you help us out."

"How?" Harrington asked, glancing at her lawyer, who nodded his approval.

"Time served," Beatrice snapped, "I wanna get out of this hell hole."

"Depends on what you have to say," Stone snapped back, "but I want it all. You tell me everything."

Cross leaned over and whispered into Stone's ear, "You can't promise that. What are you doing?"

Stone whispered back, "Go with it. I have a plan."

Stone then looked at Harrington and said, "We know everything,"

"I highly doubt that," Harrington hissed.

Stone thought for a moment, then pulled off a huge bluff, saying, "Yeah, you see, it took a while and a lot of digging, but we finally figured it out after he was killed ... Jack O'Neal was the person who murdered my father. He got off easy, but all roads still lead back to you."

A surprised look flashed across Harrington's face for a split second, and then it was gone. "Who's that? I don't know any Jack O'Neal person," Harrington replied smugly.

Cross glanced at Stone, and he said, "You know who he is, or was, rather. He's the guy you told to kill Oliver West, who worked at the coroner's office. The one and the same Oliver West who helped you out of your jam when your son died years ago by forging the autopsy report."

Harrington took the bait and, before she realized it, said, "That's not what happened! He—"

"He what?" Cross asked.

Harrington stopped mid-sentence, sat back, and smiled, saying, "You don't know anything. Do you?"

"Oh yes, we do. We know that my father was investigating something happening on the lake and suddenly my father's name appears in your secret book as knowing too much. Not long after that, my father was ambushed and murdered by somebody we now know was Jack O'Neal."

Harrington's court-appointed lawyer attempted to interject, yelling, "NOT ANOTHER—"

Harrington cut him off mid-sentence and growled, "So what? What if I did know that O'Neal killed your precious father? That has nothing to do with me!"

As soon as the words left her mouth, the court-appointed attorney lowered his head and sighed, knowing what Harrington had just done.

"What? What is it?" Harrington snapped.

Stone looked at Cross, smiled, and said, "I knew it would work."

"What are you babbling about?" Harrington snapped, "I've said nothing incriminating."

Cross smiled and said, "Actually, you did. It's called Misprision of a Felony as in 18 U.S.C. section 4 U.S. code, which is against Federal Law and could get you 3-5 more years in federal prison plus more for accessory after the fact charges and whatever else we can find."

"YOU CAN'T DO THAT!" Harrington roared as she pulled and snatched at the shackles attached to the table.

"Actually, we can, and we will!" Stone replied.

"Seems like you just talked yourself right into more charges," Cross said as they both got up and started to leave.

"WAIT! WHAT DO YOU WANT?" Harrington snapped.

Sitting back down, Stone replied, "I want to know who killed my father, why they did it, and what that has to do with what's going on out on the lake now?"

Before Harrington said a word, she looked at her court-appointed lawyer this time and waited for his approval before speaking.

"Okay, okay. I'll tell you."

"Well, we're waiting. We don't have all day," Cross snapped.

"I knew O'Neal killed your father, but I didn't have anything to do with it. That was carried out by my husband while he was still alive."

"How convenient," Cross replied. "Blame the dead guy defense."

"It's true!" Harrington replied. "Look at the handwriting in the book and compare it to mine. You'll see it does not match. My late husband wrote everything in that book! You have to believe me," Harrington pleaded.

"Oh, we believe you ... but the fact that you admitted knowing about it and you did nothing ... that does not bode well for you," Stone replied. "You might as well have shot my father yourself. GUARD!"

As Stone and Cross stood to leave again, Harrington lowered her head and said, "I'll tell you everything."

BACK AT THE sheriff's department in their war room, so to speak, FBI Special Agent Davenport had set up one of the FBI laptops, which gave him access to several databases which the Lexington County Sheriff's Department did not have.

Taking Stone's suggestion, Davenport did a deep dive on the first victim, Jeramy Donahue, which, to the casual observer, seemed to be a random killing until his name came up in connection to Jack O'Neal.

After investigating Donahue's life, he found that everything had changed when he began working for The Pearl Group in Charlotte. Since working there, Donahue went from stable to all over the map, taking extravagant trips to exotic destinations and buying cars that he couldn't afford, to say the least.

Davenport, using his powers of persuasion, called the Pearl Group and, upon making several thinly veiled FBI threats, managed to get a copy of Donahue's client list at the time of his death. Lo and behold, not one but two names stood out on his client list. "Well, I'll be damned," Davenport replied as he stared at the list.

Just then, Chief of Detectives Boone walked in and asked, "Have you heard from Stone and Cross yet?"

"Not yet. I was about to call Stone because I've found something," Davenport replied.

"So have I," Boone replied. "I can't believe what I've found."

"What is it?" Davenport asked.

Boone replied, "Jack O'Neal and Stone's father were detectives at the same time. O'Neal's name appears on more reports surrounding Lake Murray than any other back in the late eighties and early nineties. There's no proof of what I'm about to say, BUT what if O'Neal was protecting somebody that lived or worked on the lake?"

"Who?" Davenport asked.

Ignoring the question momentarily, Boone motioned toward Davenport's FBI computer and said, "I assume you have access to old investigations on that thing?"

"Mostly. Why? Who am I looking up?"

Boone smiled and said, "Take a look and tell me what you have on a Dexter Knoxx."

Once Davenport had pulled up the information on Knoxx, Boone smiled and said, "We need to call everybody and get them all gathered back here as soon as possible and put in a call to the marine unit as well. We're probably going to need their assistance. What time is it now, five o'clock?"

"Yes," Davenport replied, glancing down at his watch.

"Ok, I want everyone involved in this case, including Singh's people, at the Coroner's office in the war room at six thirty."

"For what?" Davenport asked.

Boone smiled devilishly and said, "Somebody's house of cards is about to come tumbling down." He picked up his phone and sent several texts back-to-back to Stone and Cross, telling them to meet him at a secret location.

17

When his phone rang, Dexter Knoxx was sitting outside on his massive, covered porch looking out over the lake. Looking at the name on the caller ID, he smiled when he saw that it was his son.

"Hey, Connor. How are you?" Dexter asked.

"Doing good," Connor replied. "Listen, Dad, I just got a call from the sheriff's department again, and they need my help with what's going on, so I'm going in to see what I can do. I don't know how long I'll be gone."

Dexter paused and said, "But it's late, and you know how I feel about that. I am more worried about your sobriety than anything else. You know what happens when you get under too much pressure."

"I know, Dad, but I'll be fine," Connor replied. "Besides, I have a new coping skill now ... the lake. I know if I need to, I can jump in the boat and go."

"I know, I just worry, that's all. Let me know what's going on when you can." Dexter replied.

"I will, Dad," Connor replied before hanging up the phone.

At precisely six o'clock that evening, Boone and Davenport met Cross and Stone in the baseball field parking lot off Duffle Drive, near the sheriff's department. No games were being played tonight, so the parking lot was completely empty and quiet.

As Cross and Stone pulled into the parking lot, they recognized Boone's car backed into a parking spot. Stone pulled into the adjacent spot, so her driver's door and Boone's were beside each other. Skipping the formalities, Stone rolled down the window and asked, "What's up, boss?"

"Did you get anything from Harrington?" Boone asked.

"Sure did," Stone said as she and Cross relayed what Harrington had told them.

After listening to Stone, Boone replied, "Well, that goes with what we've found out, too."

"Which is what?" Cross asked.

"Well, while you two were getting info from Harrington, Davenport and I have been compiling information on every single person involved in this case *and* on previous cases involving the lake."

"What did you find?" Stone asked.

Davenport replied, "We found several people that crossed over to several investigations, but we narrowed it down to three individuals. That said, we plan to narrow it down even further."

"And what exactly is your plan?" Stone asked.

"It starts in thirty minutes," Boone replied, "because, in thirty minutes, we're going to bring everyone who has anything to do with this case into the war room and tell them we have had a major break in the case and that the person we're after is a squatter living on the islands in the lake. We're going to play on something Connor Knoxx said a few days ago and see if we can't ruffle a feather or two."

Stone glanced at Cross, and then said, "Ok, if you say so."

"Trust me. It will make sense," Boone replied with a devious grin. "It's unconventional, but I think it will work."

"Wait a minute," Cross said, "What will this do? I fail to see how this is going to help us."

Boone replied, "Who we're after may not be a serial killer after all. It's somebody wanting us to *think* that it's a serial killer. He may be unstable and likely not all there mentally, but I don't think he's a true serial killer. The individuals that have been killed were very deliberately executed. Not because they crossed paths with a deranged person but because of what they know. Now, if the person wants us to think it's a serial killer, he will go along with what I have in store tonight."

"And the only way to truly get to the bottom of this once and for all is to identify the killer and who's paying him, and the only way to do that is to try and draw him out," Boone said.

Cross asked, "Hold up a minute ... in essence, what you're saying is that the person we're after is off his rocker and is a murderer but not a serial killer. Is that what I'm hearing?"

"Correct," Davenport replied. "The person we're after is cunning and is an expert at hiding his true identity. He's almost living a double life, and if we're right ... he will be in that room tonight."

Stone glanced at her phone and said, "Well, it's a quarter past six now, so we need to get going."

"Yep," Boone replied, "and one more thing ... not a word to anyone about this little setup since we don't know who's involved."

"Not gonna say a thing," Stone said as she glanced at Cross.

As if to read her mind, Cross said, "Only thing I have to say is, "ROLL TIDE!" to the chuckles of Davenport and Boone.

As Stone backed out of her parking spot and after they pulled off, she said, "It's the first time I've heard you talk about football or anything."

"Please ... Crimson Tide all the way, baby! ROLL TIDE!" Cross said. I know people around here are either Clemson Tigers or Gamecocks, but I would be disowned if I switched sides," Cross replied, laughing. "I might as well never go back home. ROLL TIDE is kinda like my war cry."

Fifteen minutes later, and right on time, Stone and Cross walked into the war room and found a spot beside Davenport, who was already there. A moment or two later, Boone walked in with someone nobody had seen before who, by all appearances, looked like an American Indian. He had dark brown skin and long jet-black hair neatly tied in a long ponytail reaching half the length of his back.

Even though it was warm and muggy, the stranger was dressed in a long-sleeved white button-up shirt, blue jeans, and cowboy boots.

By the time the last four entered the room, there was standing room only as there were several officers from the Lexington County Marine Unit, including Brett Gibson, who was one of the first officers on the scene when the body of Jeramy Donahue was discovered—Dr. Singh, his staff, and several SCDNR staff, including Russell Watts.

The room was abuzz with whispers of confusion, and rumors were flying from one side to the other until Boone stood at the front and exclaimed loudly, "ATTENTION, PLEASE! Settle down, and I'll make this as short and sweet as possible."

Boone paused briefly to let the crowd quiet down, then announced, "Thank you for coming out here this late. First, I want to thank everyone for your hard work and dedication since this debacle kicked off. Secondly, I want to announce that we have had a break in the case and have a person of interest in mind."

Someone from the back of the room asked, "Has there been an identification?"

"Not at this time, but one is imminent," Boone replied. "At this time, I would like Dr. William Running Bear to come up and say a few words. He is an expert on the Native Americans that used to live in this area and will be able to give us some insight into what is about to transpire."

As soon as Stone heard what was happening, she stared at Boone quizzically.

Boone made eye contact with Stone and flashed a nearly imperceptible smile before quickly looking away, trying to disguise the ruse.

The man, introduced as Dr. William Running Bear, stepped up to the front and said, "As some of you may know, tomorrow night is a full moon. For the Indians who used to roam these lands hundreds of years ago, any full moon was a sacred time. However, tomorrow night's full moon is more sacred than most due to the time of year."

"How so?" Knoxx asked.

Running Bear paused momentarily, then replied, "There is a tale from the olden days that tells of great hunts by strong Indian warriors that occur by moonlight. With the meat taken on a full moon, families would not go hungry for a long time."

"Can't do that anymore," one of the DNR men said to the cackles of the others in the room.

Unamused, Running Bear looked stone-faced and replied, "Thanks to the white man."

This brought chuckles from everyone else in the room as the game warden who commented looked down flustered.

"There are stories of a Uyaga ... evil spirit that also hunts this area. The only difference is that the Uyaga hunt warriors ... not animals. The Uyaga are powerful beings capable of taking over a man's mind and making him do the unthinkable. I have talked at length with your Chief of Detectives, Boone, and I believe whoever is doing these despicable acts on the lake is being influenced by a Uyaga."

"Why did the spirit hunt the warriors?" somebody asked.

"Because a warrior spirit is stronger than the old ones, women, and children," Running Bear replied.

"So, how do we stop him?" somebody asked.

"Uyaga only has power over a particular individual in an area. This person may be unstable, and that is how the Uyaga works. It works its way into those with broken minds and compels the person to do its bidding. Remove the person from the area, and the Uyaga loses its power."

This time, Watts spoke up and said, "I gotta say, it sounds like a whole lotta hocus pocus to me."

"Not really," Cross replied, "Where I'm from in Alabama, there are places in the bayous that even the toughest folks won't go at night because witches roam the bayous. Many folks have seen things that cannot be explained deep in the Bama bayous."

"Precisely my point," Running Bear replied. "These are mere legends, but legends are born from facts."

"So, what are we going to do?" Deputy Gibson of the Lexington County Sheriff's Marine Unit asked.

Boone smiled and said, "I'm glad you asked because we have arranged a little hunting party of our own. I have arranged it with most of your bosses except those in the coroner's office. The marine unit and multiple SCDNR boats will be out on the lake tomorrow night, stopping every boat we find, searching every island, tracking down every lead, and searching every single camp on the islands." Boone then took a stack of papers, handed it to someone in the front row, and said, "Take one and pass it around. Your assignments and partners on the water for tomorrow night's operation will be on these sheets. Make sure you are at your assigned spot at jump-off time."

"You still haven't said who we're searching for," Knoxx replied.

"It has come to our attention that there is a man who essentially lives off the grid and moves from island to island. Sadly, we do not have the name or identity of the person. We only know of this individual by visual sitings. He has an aluminum boat with a shallow draft, so he can go anywhere he wants on the lake. He has been seen near each island where a body has been found. Let me be clear: he is only a person of interest. We need to talk to this individual. Does everyone understand?"

Everyone nodded and affirmed they understood, and then Boone replied, "Good. We will set up a mobile command post on Pine Island at sunset. Does anyone have any questions?"

From the back of the room, a disembodied voice asked, "Why Pine Island?"

"Easy," Boone replied. "The premises are still being renovated, so they're off-limits to the public for now, and it's central to what's going on. You will still launch boats from the usual places. This is just where the command post will be located.

I want everyone to come prepared for war. That means come loaded for bear. I want long guns, vests, trauma kits, and tourniquets on every boat that goes out on the lake ... tomorrow night, we end this. Go home, get as much sleep as possible because tomorrow night will be an all-nighter."

As the meeting broke up and people started filing out, Boone and Running Bear hung around until they, along with Stone and Cross, were the last ones in the room.

As Stone and Cross walked up, Stone put her hands on her hips and said, "Okay, what in the hell is going on?"

"What do you mean?" Running Bear asked.

"Spill it," Stone replied firmly.

Before anyone could say anything, Cross said, "Um, pretend I don't know what's happening ... because I don't. Would someone please fill me in?"

Before anyone could say anything, Boone walked over and closed the door to the war room. Stone snapped her finger, smiled at Running Bear, and said, "Now, I know where I've seen you before. You're in a picture on Boone's desk!"

Boone and Running Bear looked at each other, and the man, introduced as Running Bear, asked, "Is it okay to talk?"

"Quietly," Boone replied.

Running Bear looked at Boone and replied, "We're cousins, and my name is actually Peter Jacobs."

"So, this was all a con job?" Cross asked.

"Yes and no," Peter replied, smiling. "Actually, I'm a Lumbee Indian from across the border in North Carolina."

"So, how much of that was bullshit you just spewed?" Cross asked.

"Oh, about fifty percent," Jacobs said, smiling. "There really were evil spirits called Uyaga's, and the rest ... well, I pulled a little from here and there."

"Are you really a doctor?" Cross asked.

"Yes, I got a doctorate from UNC Pembroke in American Indian Studies," Jacobs said proudly. "Cousin Stephen called and told me what was going on and what he needed, so I drove down."

"And I'm grateful," Boone replied. "Your performance just sewed the seed that will help us catch this guy soon ... hopefully tomorrow night."

Jacobs smiled and said, "I'll send ya my bill," before shaking everyone's hand and walking out of the conference room.

"So, what do you think?" Boone asked.

"With any luck, our killer will fall for it and try something tomorrow night during the full moon. The question is ... what?" Stone replied, worried.

"Guess we'll find out soon enough," Cross replied.

AFTER THE MEETING BROKE UP, everyone started filing out of the Sheriff's Department building and into the gated parking lot. Little did they know somebody was watching ... observing ... thinking.

Suddenly, the person took out his phone and sent a text that read:

They suspect someone. Plan B?

After a moment, the answer came back:

If you're sure ... yes.

18

The following day, members of the LCSD began prepping the command post for the night-long operation. After ensuring everything was in proper order and stocked, the Lexington County Sheriff's Department's mobile command post left the sheriff's department at six o'clock that evening, pulled onto Pine Island not long afterward, and began setting up the mobile command post.

From the time they pulled to a stop, it took less than twenty minutes for the mobile command post to become fully operational, staffed, and ready for action, just as the moon started rising over Lake Murray.

While holding a large cup of coffee, Boone climbed the steps into the mobile command post, and sat near the communication section. On the opposite wall was a large map of Lake Murray with a grid across it. The plan was straightforward. Each search boat had a corresponding map and would regularly call in their locations once they finished searching a particular area.

Then After searching that area, it would be considered clear, and someone in the command post would mark off that grid and assign them a new grid to search.

As Boone stared at the map, he began to think he had no idea what they would do if the killer didn't take the bait. Unbeknownst to all but a very few, not only was Boone tracking the operation, but he was also tracking where everyone was *within* the operation. In this way, he hoped to be able to narrow the suspect pool somewhat. Neither Boone nor anyone involved in the search knew that the person they were after was also on the lake and ... hunting them.

As darkness fell over the lake, Stone and Davenport reached their jump-off point at a marina opposite Pine Island and the command post. Before exiting Stone's car, Stone called Chief of Detectives Boone at the command post and said, "Hey, chief, it's me, Stone. Davenport and I are getting ready to head out. Is the command post ready to rock and roll?"

"All fired up and ready to go," Boone replied. "I got you and Davenport leaving from the Bush River Road and Highway Six boat ramp. Watts is picking up Cross at Siesta Cove Marina. LCSD Deputy Gibson from the marine unit is picking up Connor Knoxx from his private dock, Ooh la, la."

"Yeah, must be nice," Stone replied with a tinge of jealousy in her voice.

Boone continued, "And several other units are taking off from other marinas further west of here and working east after checking the areas around Dreher Island State Park, Fetner Island, and the Saluda River area. After checking those areas, they will start heading east, checking every spot they can until you guys flush him out, or we call the search. And, for God's sake, be careful. I wouldn't be able to handle it if something happened to one of my people."

"Aw, how sweet," Stone said as she poked a little fun at Boone, trying to lighten the mood. "Are you worried about me?"

"I'm worried about all of my people," Boone snapped. "Now get off this phone and get out on the water."

"Yes, boss," Stone said, still poking the bear somewhat, "but you can admit it; you're worried about me a little, aren't you?"

The only response Stone got was a click as Boone hung up the phone, which made Stone let out her evil little laugh.

"I know that evil laugh," Davenport replied. "What did you do?"

"Nothing, nothing at all," Stone said, smirking.

After getting out of Stone's car, the pair walked down floating docks and out to an awaiting SCDNR boat that would take them out on the lake that night. Both got settled in after introducing themselves to Game Warden Davidson, who would escort them around the lake. Davidson skillfully pushed off the dock and headed to their first assigned sector.

About the same time, Cross and Watts were pushing off from the dock at their starting point. Watts let out a long, drawn-out yawn as they pulled away from their jump-off spot. "What's the matter with you?" Cross asked.

"I just didn't get much sleep; I could never sleep during the daytime. That's all," Watts replied, as he shook his head from side to side, trying to force himself to be more alert.

"You do remember, I'm not a fan of water, right?" Cross asked.

"I remember everything," Watts said, smiling. "Speaking of remembering things, how did I get stuck with you and not Stone?"

"Safety," Cross replied.

"Oh, because I'm better at being on the lake. Is that what you mean?"

"No. I wasn't talking about my safety. I was talking about Davenport's safety because if you got Stone, it would put me with Davenport and another SCDNR guy. As much as I dislike you ... I really don't like Davenport."

"So, I'm the lesser of two evils. Is that what you're saying?" Watts asked.

Cross smiled, smacked Watts on the shoulder openhanded, and said, "Now you're getting it!"

As soon as he heard that, Watts 'accidentally' bumped the throttle too hard, causing Cross's eyes to widen and throwing Cross back onto the bench seat. "Whoops," Watts said as he looked at Cross with a devious smile.

"Asshole!" Cross muttered.

"What was that?" Watts asked, even though he knew the answer.

"I said drive the boat," Cross snapped.

As they pulled away from their jump-off point, Cross heard his name being called over the radio from the mobile command post, asking if they were on the move yet.

Cross replied, "Affirmative boss, we're on the move now. ROLL TIDE!"

This evoked several jeers from other search boats heading out onto the lake. This made Cross laugh with delight, and he said to Watts, "'Tis a good way to start this operation, by pissing off Clemson and Gamecock fans!"

Across the lake, LCSD Deputy Brett Gibson of the marine unit pulled up to the private pier at Connor Knoxx's home. Knoxx was already standing on the end of the dock waiting and hopped into the boat as Gibson skillfully pulled up with a slight tap on the dock.

After chatting momentarily, Gibson radioed the mobile command post, saying he and Knoxx were good to go.

"Outstanding!" came the reply from Boone in the mobile command post.

They all listened to radio broadcasts as each boat checked in one by one, saying they were leaving their assigned jump-off position or had already left and were on the move.

It wasn't long before everyone could hear stops being made over the radio and different boat registration numbers being called in as most boaters were heading back to their marinas for the night.

Shortly, Davenport and Stone reported making their first contact, but only a few fishermen and nothing more.

In the command post, Boone monitored the radio calls while several other officers checked the identifications of all the people they stopped and entered their registration numbers.

Boone then heard Watts calling in, saying they spotted a boat near Bomb Island and were heading to intercept it. Immediately, Boone radioed back, asking, "Is the boat running?"

"No, it doesn't appear to be," Watts replied. "We just haven't gotten close enough to effect a stop yet. Stand by."

After a few tense moments of silence from Watts, Boone replied, "Watts report ... Watts report in. What's going on?"

NOT LONG AFTER being picked up at his home, the boat, driven by LCSD Gibson of the marine unit and Connor Knoxx, started into the lake. "You do remember that I am in no way, shape, or fashion a cop, and I do not have arresting powers. Right?" Knoxx asked.

"Yeah, I remember," Gibson replied. That's okay, though. I don't think we'll run into any trouble. Personally, I think this is all a wild goose chase."

"Why do you say that?" Knoxx asked.

Gibson replied, "Because this lake is so damn big, there's no way a search with a dozen boats will catch this guy. There are too many places to hide, especially at night."

"Yeah, I understand, but they can't catch this guy on paper either. There's no evidence anywhere, so they're getting desperate. They feel like they have to do something, I guess."

Gibson radioed that they were at the start of their designated search grid and were about to begin their search. Shortly thereafter, they saw lights from a boat in the distance and motored over to investigate.

As the pair motored over, they saw that it was merely a couple of fishermen packing up from a day of fishing. After checking their identifications and boat registration, the fishermen thanked the deputy for checking on them.

Back in the command post, Boone and the people with him were busy monitoring transmissions from different areas of the lake. The entire operation went silent as people listened in as the command post tried to re-establish communications with Watts and Cross."

"Mobile Command Post to SCDNR Watts, respond immediately," came a voice over the radio.

After a tense pause, everyone recognized Watts' voice over the radio, saying, "Sorry about that boss. We were in the middle of talking to a boater we had just stopped."

Everyone breathed a sigh of relief as the command post acknowledged their transmission and reminded them to check in when they found something.

The search went on hour after hour, with the search teams checking every small inlet and island they could and shining spotlights into the shallowest and narrowest of places they couldn't get to on a boat, hoping and waiting for something to happen.

Finally, sometime after midnight, the search teams caught a break.

While stopping and checking registrations, people on a sailboat told Watts and Cross about a small aluminum boat that duck hunters use, sitting deep in the shallow cove on Misty Island. The people on the sailboat relayed to Watts that the only way they saw it was because the running lights were on, but as long as they were in sight of the boat, it wasn't moving. Cross and Watts talked it over, thanked the sailboat owners, and considered this to be a solid lead. Cross said they would definitely check it out.

Meanwhile, near the middle of the lake, Stone, Davenport, and SCDNR Davidson had just finished checking out a camping spot on Jim Spence Island and were returning to the boat when they heard a garbled and frantic radio call over the airways, "Emergency ... backup! Man down..."

19

A t that moment, two critical things happened. First, the entire radio channel the operation was on went completely silent as everyone strained to listen for more details and prepared to act as soon as they received more information on who was in trouble.

Secondly, at almost the exact same moment across the lake in the command post, everyone who just moments before was sleepy and rubbing their eyes was now wide awake and on point, standing by, waiting to assess the situation and send teams to the people in trouble.

Boone grabbed the microphone from the person seated at the radio and nearly shouted into the radio, "Whoever sent the distress call, report! What's the situation? Report, damn it!"

After a long pause, everyone could hear heavy breathing and the faint words ... "Misty Island."

Boone practically screamed into the microphone, "MISTY ISLAND! GO! GO!"

Stone looked at Davidson and asked, "How far away is that?"

"Over six miles away," Davidson replied.

"How long before we could get there?" Stone pleaded.

"Over six miles, at night, eleven to twelve minutes."

Stone yelled into the radio, "Mobile command, is there anyone else who can get to them faster? We're twelve minutes away!"

"Not at this time. Other boats are closer, but they're either checking on islands or deep in the shallows. You're it! Now get moving!"

LCSD Gibson grabbed the mic and said, "We're further away, but we'll be right behind you as backup! We will be about five minutes behind you!"

Stone looked at Davidson and said, "You heard the man. Punch it!"

"Hang on tight! This is about to be a wild ride! Davenport, get low in the bow and keep a sharp watch for running lights off our bow!"

"Will do!" Davenport replied as he scampered up to the bow of the boat. Once there, he squatted down for protection, sticking his head above the bow, and said, "Hit it!"

When Davenport gave him the word, Davidson jammed the throttles forward, and the boat lept out of the water. Moments later, they were rocketing across the middle of the lake at night and had no idea what they were running into.

BEFORE LONG, the boat that Davidson was driving eased off the power and approached Misty Island as fast as he dared.

Stone and Davenport lept ashore as soon as the boat's bow grounded along the island's edge, pausing only long enough for Davenport to pull out and chamber a round in the tactical twelve-gauge shotgun they brought for added firepower. Davidson secured the boat and quickly followed a few steps behind.

Once on the island, all three stopped momentarily to get their bearings and see if they could hear movement anywhere. Barely above a whisper, Stone asked, "Davidson, have you ever been here before?"

"Once or twice ... in the daytime, never at night," he replied softly.

Davenport said, "Okay, let's fan out a little, but stay close."

"Listen, be careful. This place has undergrowth and some trees, but it's pretty clean and open ... during the day, that is ... so far, since it's night I can't see shit."

Before separating, Stone took out her phone, turning the brightness low, and tried to send Cross a text telling him they were on the island and asking him to respond. However, no response came.

"We need to start clearing this island and do it now," Stone said, deeply concerned. "My partner's in trouble."

Slowly and ever-so quietly, the trio left the shore where the boat was and fanned out until there were five yards of separation between each of them.

All three cautiously moved forward, sweeping the area before them with their flashlights as they searched for clues to what may have happened. Since the emergency call, there had been no contact from either Cross or Watts, and the uncertainty magnified with each passing second.

Finally, the three had cleared part of one end of the island and found nothing. By then, the boat driven by LCSD Gibson and Connor Knoxx could be heard approaching the island.

The trio briefly considered attempting to clear the rest of the island but decided to wait for Gibson and Knoxx to arrive before proceeding for fear of missing something. Davidson signaled to the fast-approaching boat with his flashlight, and in a few minutes, Gibson had expertly beached his boat right where the group was.

After securing their boat, Gibson asked, "What's the situation?"

Stone replied, "We've cleared the portion of the island to our left, but we still have not seen or heard anything from our missing people. We were about to start moving left when we heard you approaching. We figured it would be better to wait until you got here and go with at least one more gun."

"Sound decision," Gibson replied. "Let's move out."

Now, the search party of five fanned out, with Knoxx slightly behind the others since he was technically not law enforcement and not armed. Now able to fan out even wider, the search party slowly and methodically worked their way across the island until they could see Watts' boat tied up not far away, opposite where the rescue team had come ashore.

As the team reached the area where Cross and Watts had come ashore, they saw tracks leading towards a part of the island with what appeared to be more dense vegetation. Just then, Stone's phone buzzed.

As soon as she looked at the phone, she saw a one-word text from Boone in the command center:

REPORT!

Stone replied that they had found the boat but nothing else so far, and she would report when she had something.

"Ok, the answer is in that direction," Stone said as she pointed toward the area they had yet to clear. "Let's move out."

The team moved quickly and methodically toward the end of the island they had yet to search. However, what they found proved to be more of a mystery than anything else because, in the end ... they found absolutely nothing.

After they realized they were the only ones on the island, Davenport asked, "Wait a minute! What in the hell is going on here? Did we miss something?"

"No," Knoxx replied. "I know this island. There's nowhere to hide, so we would have found them or their bodies if they were here."

"Well, what in the hell happened?" Knoxx asked.

"I think I know what happened, and you won't believe it," Stone replied as she grabbed her cell phone and called Boone at the mobile command center.

"What are you thinking?" Knoxx asked.

Before she could respond, Boone answered his phone in the mobile command center, saying, "What in the hell's going on? Who's down?"

Stone replied, "We just finished clearing the island, and they're not here. They're gone."

"They're gone! What in the hell do you mean they're gone?" Boone snapped.

"I mean, Watts' boat is here, but they're not. They're just gone," Stone replied. "They've been taken."

"Taken! Taken how?" Boone nearly shouted through the phone.

"I don't know, but that's the only thing that makes sense right now," Stone replied, "We've searched the entire island, and they are not here."

Boone replied, "Okay, two things. First, I will send out a BOLO for anything moving on the lake that's not in our search party. Secondly, I'm sending more boats to you as we speak to aid in the search."

Before Stone could reply, she heard the call go out over the airwaves, and multiple boats replied that they were making their way to Misty Island at the fastest possible speed. Before long, several more boats had arrived at Misty Island to see what they could do to aid in the search-turned-rescue operation.

When the sun started rising over the lake, several more boats arrived and were immediately dispatched to nearby Timmons Island, Holiday Island, and Hollow Cay in search of the two missing men. Eventually, a search team found a shallow-draft aluminum boat with its bow grounded in a small cove, which was only a short walk through the woods from Campground Road.

When Boone heard this in the mobile command center, he slammed his hand down on the counter in frustration and said, "DAMN IT! Someone could take them anywhere from there!" After taking a few breaths and regaining his composure, Boone called Stone on the radio and told her to go over every square inch of Misty Island and Watts' boat.

One hour later, Stone called Boone from her cellphone, turned on the speaker phone so Davenport could hear what was being said, and asked, "Well, has anyone found anything yet?"

"Not since they found that boat a while ago. Tell me you have something," Boone replied.

"Well, yes and no," Stone said.

"What in the hell kind of answer is that?" Boone replied.

"I haven't found anything, no blood, signs of a scuffle, or anything that tells me they put up a fight, which is strange. I mean, you know how big Cross is. There is no way someone took him down without a fight, much less him *and* Watts, unless ..." Stone trailed off.

"Unless what?" Boone asked, "I can almost see those wheels in your head turning. What are you thinking?"

Stone took a deep breath and said, "If someone managed to knock both of them out, there would be drag marks somewhere, but there aren't any. What in the hell am I missing?"

"Maybe you're not missing anything," Davenport replied.

Through the phone, Boone replied, "What are you talking about?"

"Yes, please elaborate," Stone replied.

Without answering directly, Davenport asked, "That boat that was found pushed up in the woods nearby, where is it right now?"

"I have a GPS location on it. I can send it to you," Boone shot back.

"Do it," Davenport replied, "because if the answer isn't here on Misty Island, it has to be there with the other boat."

"I don't even know if this boat the search party found has anything to do with what's happening. For all we know, it's just somebody's little boat to tootle around the cove in. There's no way to know if it's connected or not."

"It's connected," Davenport replied. "It has to be."

Within moments, Boone had sent Stone the location of where the boat had been found, and Stone, Davenport and Davidson headed for the second boat while everyone else kept searching Misty Island and the surrounding islands nearby.

With the sun now fully up and shining brightly over Lake Murray, Stone and Davenport grabbed Davidson, who had been driving them around the lake, and headed toward the grounded boat the search team found nearby.

Ten minutes later, Davidson pulled into the small cove, and as they entered the cove, they could see two more boats already near their target. When they pulled up, Stone could see the long faces of some of the officers present and asked, "What? What did you find?"

Somberly, one of the men that Stone did not know too well, replied, "We've found blood and drag marks. Not a lot of blood ... but still."

"Show me," Stone said, still seated inside Davidson's boat.

One of the men pointed to the bottom of the boat near the bow and said, "There are several small smears of blood here, and a few drops scattered around and another up on the lip of the bow. There are drag marks leaving the boat and heading into the woods, where we lose them a few feet into the dense vegetation."

Davenport hopped out of the boat onto shore and carefully followed the drag marks for as long as he could until he lost them in the thick underbrush, just like the other officers said. Still, instead of stopping, he continued on roughly the same trajectory that the drag marks were heading in to see if he could pick up the trail anywhere else further along the way.

Davenport returned a few minutes later, swatting at bugs, and said, "Well, I know it's not conclusive, but I did find some broken branches further in that direction, which tends to indicate something big went through there recently."

With a huff, Stone replied, "Great, just great. They could be anywhere, but this still makes no sense at all. Who would have the ability to abduct someone like Cross and Watts?"

Davenport stood there momentarily without answering, then said, "Maybe they didn't."

"What? Maybe who didn't?" Stone asked. "I know it's still early. We've been up all night and exhausted, but you are not making any sense right now."

Davenport snapped, "Give me Boone's number. I need to talk to him."

"Just use mine," Stone replied.

"No, mine is a government phone. I know it's secure. Trust me, it will make sense in a few minutes."

Stone relayed the number, and Davenport dialed as she called it out. Moments later, they heard, "Boone hear," through the speakerphone on Davenport's phone.

Davenport replied, "Chief Boone, this is Davenport calling from my secure phone. I need you to do me a favor and give me the number to SCDNR. I need to talk to somebody in charge over there immediately."

Boone relayed the number, and Davenport thanked him, hung up, and immediately redialed the number Boone had given him.

When someone picked up, Davenport said, "This is Special Agent Peter Davenport with the FBI. I need to talk to someone who can give me GPS tracking information on one of your boats for the past twenty-four hours. This is part of the ongoing investigation on the lake, and I need this information immediately."

Stone could not hear what the person asked, but she heard Davenport reply ... "SCDNR Russell Watts."

20

"WATTS?" Stone nearly shouted, "you cannot be serious!"

"It's the only thing that makes sense," Davenport replied. "There is no evidence of anyone else being on that island except for those two, and it would have taken several men to take down Cross unless Watts took him out from behind while they were on the boat, which explains the small amount of blood."

"But ... it can't be Watts," Stone said, shocked.

"I hope I'm wrong ... but I just don't think so," Davenport replied.

Before Stone could respond, Davenport began dialing a number from his saved list, told the person who he was, and said, "I need to know everything there is to know about Russell Watts with the South Carolina Department of Natural Resources, and I need it sent to my phone as soon as possible." Without waiting for a response, Davenport hung up the phone and said, "Let's get out of here."

"How long will it take before we hear back from whoever you just called?" Stone asked.

"Five or ten minutes," Davenport replied.

"What?" Stone said, shocked, "How in the hell can ..."

Davenport smiled devilishly and said, "Magic."

Stone called Boone back on her phone and said, "You won't believe this, but we may have a lead. Get some people ready to roll out at a moment's notice should we need them."

"Um, ok, fine, but you wanna tell me what in the hell is going on?" Boone replied.

"Not right now, I want to be absolutely sure first," Stone said.

Boone took a deep breath and said, "Okay ... the ball is in your court, roll with it. I will back you one hundred percent."

Stone replied, "Thanks, boss," and hung up her phone. After putting her phone back in her pocket, Stone called Davidson over to where she and Davenport stood and said, "Davenport and I have a lead. We need you to get us back to the marina where our car is as quickly as possible."

Davidson smiled and said, "Good thing, I love driving fast! Hop aboard, and let's blow this joint!"

~

FROM THE MOMENT HE AWOKE, Cross realized he was tied up in what appeared to be a metal chair of some sort, with his hands and arms bound behind the chair with nylon rope usually associated with boating. He had a black hood covering his head so he could not see his surroundings. Since the hood was covering his head, he chose to remain perfectly still, hoping his captor would not realize he had regained consciousness.

Even though his head was swimming like he had been out binge drinking the previous night, he was willing himself to remember what had led up to his capture. He had no idea where he was or if Watts was around, but he knew one thing ... it was not good.

One moment, he was searching the boat he and Watts had discovered when suddenly, he felt a sharp jab to his neck, and the next thing he knew, he was here ... wherever here was.

Once he felt he had regained his faculties, Cross said, "Yo, Watts, are you here?"

After a brief pause, Cross heard Watts reply softly, "Yeah, I'm here. What ... what's going on? I can't see anything. I'm tied up somehow."

"Neither can I," Cross replied. "Do you remember anything?"

After a brief pause, Watts replied, "No. One moment, I was covering you while you were on the boat, and the next, I was here."

"That's what happened to me, too," Cross replied. "How could somebody have taken us both out like this?"

"I don't know, but I feel like I've been hit by a truck," Watts replied, breathing heavily.

"I know what you mean," Cross replied with a slight chuckle. "I haven't felt this bad since my college days."

"Ugh, don't remind me," Watts replied. "What in the hell is this all about? Why would someone do something so risky? I mean, why kidnap two people like this, much less officers?"

"It would seem that we made some sort of impression on somebody," Cross replied, trying to lighten the mood slightly.

"I'm supposed to be the funny guy," Watts replied, "although I don't feel like being the funny guy right now." After a pause, Watts continued, "So, what do you think is going on?"

Cross took a deep breath and said, "I think the serial killer set a trap for us. That's what I think."

Watts replied sarcastically, "I'm not a detective or anything, but since we've both been knocked out, blindfolded, and tied to chairs, I'd say you are right. The question is, what do we do about it?"

"I'm not sure there's anything we can do about it," Cross replied.

"Think, man!" Watts replied as fear started creeping into his voice. "You must know something that will help!"

"I'm thinking!" Cross snapped. "We believe it's someone close to the investigation, but we can't figure it out. We also believe this had something to do with some things that happened in the past, but we've been unable to put all the pieces together. I know who would be a great candidate for the killer, but we don't have enough evidence yet."

"Who do you think?" Watts asked. "Wait! Don't tell me, let me guess, you believe it's Connor Knoxx, don't you?"

"He checks all the boxes for sure," Cross replied. "Were you thinking the same thing, or did you have someone else in mind?"

Suddenly, the wood floor creaking told Cross that someone was moving around in the room. Pausing to listen, Cross said, "Don't say another word, Watts. We're not alone."

Cross' mind raced as he struggled against the chair and to listen for anything that could give a clue as to who may be in the room with them. The footsteps came closer and closer to Cross as he strained with all his might against the restraints that would not budge.

Finally, the footsteps stopped close enough to Cross that he could hear the person breathing. "Who the hell are you?" Cross roared. "Knoxx, is that you? Take these restraints off, and let's see how big and bad you really are!" Cross snarled, "I'll twist that little chicken neck right off your shoulders!"

Suddenly, the cover was violently yanked off Cross' head, with the opening of the cover raking across Cross' face, reopening the cut on his lip and scraping across the tip of his nose and his eyes.

Cross blinked his eyes several times before he could see well enough to believe what he was seeing. "You!" Cross sneered as he looked around at his surroundings.

"That's right ... amigo. It's me," Watts said as he squatted in front of Cross to look him directly in the eye.

"Why? Why in the hell would you do this?" Cross asked in complete shock.

"Because my employer pays me very well, and some things that have happened on and around this lake can never get out," Watts said with an evil demonic snicker that shook Cross to his core. "Consider me the ... caretaker of the lake's secrets."

"Man, what in the hell are you talking about?" Cross asked slowly. "You don't believe that load of crap about the Indian witch, do you?"

Cross was immediately struck with a violent backhand across his face, snapping his head back and splitting his lip open even further. "I know the legend is real because I've seen the witch," Watts replied with an evil grin as he stared into Cross' eyes, trying to peer into his soul.

"What in the hell do you mean you've seen this witch?" Cross asked, trying to keep Watts talking.

With unblinking eyes, Watts recounted the time on Goat Island when he saw the exquisite red glowing eyes and how he was told to bring sacrifices to the islands or everyone would face the consequences.

As he spoke about what he had seen, Watts grinned and looked into the distance, recalling what happened that night with total adoration.

Cross sat there listening to Watts, and when he could, Cross said, "Watts, man, you need some help. Let me get you some help. Come on, man, let me help you," Cross practically pleaded.

Instead of answering, Watts let out an evil giggle, making Cross' blood run cold. Then Watts slowly stood and walked over to a table in the corner of the room, where he picked up a sheathed hunting knife. He pulled the sheath off, dropped it on the table, and slowly walked back over to where Cross was in the center of the room.

Watts slowly circled Cross as he let the point of the knife slowly drag across his shoulder, the base of his neck, and across to his other shoulder.

"Watts, come on, man! You know, we're cool! All that stuff about me messing with you was me playing around with you, that's all." Cross said as he scanned the surroundings, desperately looking for a way out. He was unsure of his location, but he appeared to be in an older-model mobile home. The windows were covered with paper, but in one corner, where the paper was torn, he could see only trees and nothing else. He could see nothing useful at all in determining his whereabouts. It wouldn't matter if he knew since he was tied up in a chair and couldn't escape.

"It doesn't matter now," Watts replied softly as he continued to circle Cross, letting the knife's point drag across his shoulders as he walked behind Cross.

"Wait! Wait!" Cross pleaded, trying to keep Watts talking, "What did you mean when you said your employer paid you well? How can a supernatural witch pay you to do things?"

Watts stopped circling Cross and again squatted down in front of him so he could look Cross directly in the eyes and said, "My employer is of this world, but my helper ... is not. Tell me, do you know how the Indians that used to live in this area would dispatch deer they wounded?"

"No, but I believe you're about to tell me," Cross replied.

"In days gone by, once the deer was hit with an arrow, the Indians would track it until it dropped, then dispatch it with two quick jabs of the knife between the ribs on a deer into the heart and lungs to finish it off quickly. This was done to prevent injury to the warrior from the deer's antlers. Does this sound ... familiar to you?"

Cross muttered, "Two knife wounds to the right side. Yeah, it's familiar. Let me guess, you're right-handed."

"Yes, indeed," Watts said as he held up his right hand, slowly waving the hunting knife back and forth in front of Cross, "I guess I should thank you, though, before ..."

"Thank me for what?" Cross asked, trying everything he could to keep Watts talking.

"I should thank you for telling me about the investigation. My plan is working perfectly. I knew you would automatically assume it was Knoxx, leaving me free to continue my work. With that being said, I think our time is coming to an end ... amigo."

Cross watched wild-eyed as Watts stood up smiling and once again started circling him like a Great White getting ready to attack his next meal. Sensing impending doom, Cross once again struggled in vain against the ropes as Watts walked around Cross for the final time.

As Watts stood behind the chair restraining the tied-up Cross, he asked, "Do you have any final words?"

"Who is your employer? If you're going to kill me ... you owe me that much!"

Watts leaned over and started to whisper something into Cross' ear, but before he could say anything, several nearby windows suddenly shattered as multiple flashbang grenades bounced into the room and rolled around.

Before either Cross or Watts could do anything, three nearly simultaneously deafening explosions and blinding flashes permeated the room. Almost at the same instant, the door of the mobile home crashed open, and several SWAT team members quickly rushed in, followed by Stone and Davenport.

Before Stone or Davenport could react, one of the assaulting SWAT team members stitched three bullets in the center of Watts' chest, ensuring he was dead before he had a chance to do anything.

Stone raced over to the unconscious and bleeding Cross, all the while yelling, "MEDIC! I NEED A MEDIC IN HERE NOW!"

As the medics who had been waiting nearby bounded up the steps and into the mobile home, Stone pulled out a knife and, as quickly as possible, began cutting the large ropes that kept the unconscious Cross in the chair.

The medics lowered Cross to the ground as gently as possible and began administering first aid to the stricken detective. Within minutes, Cross was sitting up, taking deep breaths from an oxygen mask provided by the medics while they took his vitals.

Cross pulled the mask down and, for the first time, was able to give a little smirk and asked, "What took you so long?"

"You just put that mask back on. It's over," Stone said reassuringly.

"No ... it's not ... over," Cross muttered.

"What? What do you mean it's not over?" Stone asked as she looked at Davenport with concern.

"Somebody else is ... involved, and I know who it is," Cross said as he struggled to talk.

21

L ater that night, while Cross was resting in a private room in the hospital, he watched as a spokesman for the Lexington County Sheriff's Department gave a carefully crafted account of the rescue mission that had transpired earlier in the day and what was known about the serial killer.

As he watched, Stone and Davenport walked into the room, and Stone asked, "How ya feeling, big guy?"

Cross said, "My ears are still ringing a little, and I feel like I've been hit by a truck, but I'm going to be all right. Doctors want to keep me overnight to make sure there are no lasting effects. How many flash bangs did SWAT use? Damn!"

Stone smiled and said, "We wanted to ensure he was disoriented enough to give us time to get in. Besides, we knew you could handle it, ya big baby."

"So, what do you know?" Cross asked.

Stone looked at Davenport and said, "Go ahead, you tell him. We would not have found him in time if it weren't for you and the FBI."

"Tell me what?" Cross asked.

"After today's events, we did a deep dive into Russell Watts' entire life, and you won't believe what we found."

"What?" Cross asked.

"After the rescue and once we knew you would be all right, we secured warrants and went to his house. It took a while, but we found a treasure trove of information and papers hidden in a floor safe under a piece of furniture in his home."

"And what exactly did you find? Before you guys got there, Watts said his employer paid him very well. Who was his employer?"

"You won't believe me when we tell you," Stone said with a smirk.

"Who?" Cross asked.

Ignoring the question, Stone asked, "Are you going to be good getting out of here tomorrow?"

Cross sat up and replied, "I'm good to go now! Roll Tide!"

Stone put her arm on his shoulder, saying, "Whoa there, easy, big guy. You still gotta stay overnight for observation, but you'll be in on the takedown as long as the doctor says you can go. Besides, it will take us a bit to get things set up, which will give you more time to recover. We'll be back first thing in the morning to get you."

"You promise?" Cross asked.

Smiling, Stone said, "Yes, we promise."

"Good, because if you stand me up ... I won't be pleased," Cross grinned. "Now get out. I gotta get some sleep. We have a big day tomorrow."

THE FOLLOWING MORNING, Stone and Davenport went to the hospital to pick up Cross, who was already dressed when they arrived. As soon as they walked in, Cross asked, "Since I had to put the same clothes back on from yesterday, I don't suppose we could make a quick pit stop, could we?"

"I think we have time," Stone said, smiling, thinking she was glad to see Cross up and moving around.

Thirty minutes after leaving the hospital, Cross walked back out of his apartment after taking a quick shower and changing into fresh clothes. After he jumped back in the car Cross asked, "Now what?"

Stone looked at him in the mirror and said, "Now, we go make an arrest, that's what."

"And we're going to do that with just the three of us?" Cross asked.

Stone let out an evil little giggle and said, "Not exactly, you'll see."

Twenty minutes later, Stone was pulling up to the gate on Dexter Knoxx's property. As they approached the gate, they saw multiple sheriff and SWAT vehicles.

As Stone's car came to a stop near the staging sheriff's vehicles, everyone started clapping when they saw Cross was okay. Boone walked over and shook hands with the big man, then asked, "You ready for this?"

"Hell yeah, I'm ready," Cross said, smiling.

"All you gotta do is give the word then," Boone replied, handing Cross a portable radio.

Cross grinned, pushed the button on the side, and said into the microphone, "ROLL TIDE! EXECUTE! EXECUTE! EXECUTE!"

Within moments of the execution order being given, Lexington County's armored Bearcat led the charge, bursting through the security gate and barreling down the long drive toward the main house with SWAT and other patrol cars swiftly following behind in a massive show of force considering they had no idea what they would be walking into.

On the lake, several Lexington County Sheriff boats from the marine unit docked at the pier, hoping to cut off any escape by water. Nobody realized there was another way out of Dexter's compound ... one that not even Connor knew about.

When Dexter realized what was happening, he scampered to a smaller, secondary dock across the property, opposite the main dock that Connor uses. Dexter had paid someone years ago to add extra height to the smaller dock purposefully because it was a perfect place to keep a hidden personal watercraft for emergencies, just like now.

Dexter ran out onto the dock, lifted a small trap door, and, in moments, was rocketing across the lake, being pursued by the Lexington County Marine patrol boats.

Back on the property, several units converged on the main house while SWAT and detectives descended on the guest house where Connor Knoxx lived and took him into custody without incident.

As Stone, Davenport, and Cross entered the guest house, Connor asked, shocked, "What in the hell is going on? Why are you chasing my dad? I've been working with you to help figure this out. Remember, or have you forgotten already?"

Stone said, "Did you see the press conference about who the serial killer was yesterday after we rescued Cross?"

Connor said, "Yes, I saw it. Why? What does that have to do with me or my father?"

Davenport replied, "We found a treasure trove of evidence that tells us Russell Watts had been working for your father for years and was your father's ... shall we say handyman, for problems."

"I did not know any of that. My father always told me he was retired." Conner replied calmly.

"And technically speaking, you're right," Davenport replied. "As far as we know, your father has not been active in any business for years. Tell me ... where would he go?"

"I don't know," Connor said emphatically.

"You must know something," Stone said.

"I don't! I don't know anything. You saw what just happened; he abandoned me and ran. I can tell you that he's always said he has money in offshore accounts, but I have no idea where or how much. Look around. This place is all I know."

Just then, a call came over the airways for Stone to go to the main house. She left Davenport and Cross with Connor and said, "If he says anything about what is happening on the lake, relay it to the boats and other units. Hopefully, we can end this before anyone else gets hurt."

"We will," Cross replied.

Stone walked outside and jogged over to the main house, up the steps, and into an office where Boone was standing, going through some papers on Dexter's desk. "Did you find something boss?"

"I'll say I did," Boone replied as he handed Stone a typed piece of paper.

Stone grabbed the paper and read what amounted to a complete confession, laying out everything that had happened and why for the police, not to mention completely exonerating Connor.

After reading the paper, Stone said aloud to no one in particular, "Oh, what a tangled web we weave."

"Tell me about it," Boone replied.

"What's going on with the chase? Have they caught him yet?"

"Not only have they not caught him, they can't even find him right now. That personal watercraft was heavily modified, and with its shallow draft, the first thing he did was head into shallow water where our boats couldn't go."

"Don't tell me he's gone," Stone said.

Boone replied, "Last I heard, they had lost sight of him, but they, along with SCDNR boats, were still looking. We tried to get a helicopter, but the cloud ceiling was too low."

"Where did he go?" Stone asked.

Boone replied, "At last report, he was running straight into the shallows of the Saluda River."

"Damn!" Stone said. "What do you want to do about Connor?"

"Do we have anything on him?" Boone asked.

"No, nothing," Stone replied. "If anything, he has helped in every way he could. I truly believe he is not involved."

"Okay then, give me time to make some calls and figure this out. Go back and see if Connor will tell you anything about where his father might go."

"Will do, boss," Stone said as she headed for the door to return to the guest house.

When Stone returned, she walked into the door, and as soon as Connor laid eyes on her, he asked, "Did they catch my father yet? Is it over?"

"I'm afraid they haven't caught him yet. When they last saw him, he was headed up into the shallows of the Saluda River. If you know anything, you have to tell me." Stone pleaded.

"I'm sorry, but I don't know anything. There are things about my father that I don't even know. He made plans without me, or I would be with him. I can't believe he left me." Connor said as he dropped his head in disbelief.

Stone said, "My boss found what amounts to be a complete confession in your dad's office. This confession exonerates you entirely as long as your name doesn't appear anywhere in your dad's files as being a willing participant."

"It won't," Connor assuredly replied. "Wait, what's going to happen to me now? Will I be able to stay here?"

"I don't see why not," Stone said, "but that will ultimately be up to people higher up the food chain than me. Are you telling me the truth about not knowing where your father is going or what his plans are?"

"Absolutely," Connor replied, "with my mental health issues after the war, there's no way I could be locked up. I feel locked up in here. The only place I feel free is out there on the water. I wouldn't risk losing that for anything."

Davenport glanced at Cross, then stared at Connor, momentarily cracked a thin smile, and said, "You know, I actually believe you."

"And so do I," Stone replied. "We'll probably be here all day and into the night. Anything you can tell us would go a long way in the eyes of the law for you."

Connor said, "I honestly don't know anything. Feel free to look anywhere you like and ask any questions you want. Look, he just abandoned me here to fend for myself. I'm not exactly happy with him right now."

Stone said, "And rightfully so. Listen, we'll be here for a while like I said, so if you need anything today, tomorrow, or anytime, don't hesitate to reach out. I know some great counselors that have helped many veterans like yourself."

"Thank you, but I've had enough counselors to last a lifetime. All the therapy I need is right out there," Connor said, as he pointed out to the lake.

"We'll get you out there as soon as possible," Stone said. "Anyway, we gotta go over to the main house. Again, if you need anything, don't hesitate to ask."

"I won't," Connor said as he walked Stone, Cross, and Davenport to the guest house door.

Before leaving, Cross turned around, stood as tall as his massive frame would allow, and said, "Listen ... if I find one shred of evidence that you were anywhere near my kidnapping, I'm going to come back over here, and I'm going to put the cuffs on you myself, and I'm going to squeeze them so tight that we're going to have to cut them off of you. Do you understand?"

Connor put on a brave face and replied, "I understand, but it won't come to that."

"For your sake, I hope you're right," Cross said as he reached out and shook hands with Connor before all three turned and walked away.

As they walked around to the main house, Davenport said, "Poor guy, I can't help but feel for him."

Stone replied, "Yeah, I know. He can't help who his father is or what the war did to him."

Ignoring their statements, Cross said, "Come on, we're burning daylight. I don't want to be out here any longer than I have to be. I need a beer."

"That's the best thing I've heard all day. The first round is on me when we get there," Stone said.

"Well, we have a long way to go before we get there, so let's start turning this place upside down," Cross replied with his patented smile.

The team found a virtual treasure trove scattered throughout Dexter Knoxx's office and a hidden wall safe in another part of the house that Connor had told law enforcement about.

Later that day, as the sun went down, Stone walked back to the guest house and knocked on the door one final time. Connor opened the door, and before he could say anything, Stone said, "Well, apparently, your father knows the lake pretty well. He managed to evade our people for the time being."

"You don't think he will return here, do you?" Connor asked. "I mean, am I okay with being here still?"

"Yes, we've gotten word from the higher-ups, and for now, you're good. We will take your passport, and officers will come by occasionally to ensure he doesn't return. I even managed to let you keep your boat and the keys, provided you do not go out on camping trips for the time being. Other than that, the place is all yours for now."

"That's a tough one, but I think I can manage ... as long as I can go fishing," Connor said with a smile.

"Day trips only," Stone said.

"Agreed," Connor replied.

EPILOGUE

The first night with the entire property to himself was a long and lonely night for Connor. He watched television and generally tried to keep himself busy, finally falling asleep on the couch with the TV on somewhere after two o'clock in the morning.

Shortly before six the next morning, he was awakened by someone who turned out to be a Lexington County Sheriff checking the grounds to ensure Dexter did not double back for any reason. After checking the grounds and finding nothing, the deputy drove around the property with his spotlights on and then slowly left.

Later that morning, after a line of rainstorms had passed, Connor loaded his fishing equipment into his bass boat and left for a day of fishing. Unbeknownst to him, Stone and Cross were sitting nearby with a view of his dock, watching him go.

"Whatcha wanna do?" Cross asked as they watched him pull off.

"Nothing. We'll wait for him to return, and then we'll chat with him. Maybe he'll slip up," Stone said. "It's the only thing we've got for now."

"Is the tracker working?" Cross asked.

"Working like a champ," Stone said with a smile, "We'll be able to follow him wherever he goes. As long as he's with the boat, we will know where he is."

Later that afternoon, Stone and Cross watched a blip on a small screen coming back towards their location. Cross left their hiding spot on the road and pulled back onto the property as the blip approached their location. Cautiously pulling the car out of the line of sight so Connor would not see them, Cross and Stone waited for Connor to dock the boat and begin walking up toward the guest house before showing themselves.

When Connor saw the two detectives, he smiled and asked, "Did you come by to check up on me? If so, I'm doing fantastic. The bass were biting, and I couldn't miss after that rainstorm earlier today."

"That's good, Connor. Yes, we did come by to check on you. We wanted to see how you are doing and to ensure everything is okay."

"Everything's simply ... fantastic," Connor said with a smile. I learned from my father's lawyer that this place is paid for, I'm in the clear; all I have to do is keep the taxes paid, and I can go fishing anytime. Speaking of my father, have you found him?"

Cross looked at Stone and then said, "Not yet, but we will."

"I hope you do." Connor replied, "I hope you do."

Over the next few days, Connor Knoxx went fishing almost every day, and nearly every day, a Lexington County Sheriff or a detective came by to check on him.

The following week, Stone and Cross drove onto the property. After parking and exiting their vehicle, they knocked on the door to the guest house. This time, Connor never came to the door. Instead, from behind them, they heard Connor call out, "I'm over here!"

Both turned to see Connor walking out of the main house with a broad smile. As Stone and Cross walked over, Connor said, "I decided to move over to the main house. That way, I can rent the guest house as an Airbnb."

"Wise choice," Stone replied with a forced smile.

"What is it? What's going on?" Connor asked.

Cross looked at Stone, and since she was the ranking detective, it became her job to deliver the news. "Yesterday, boaters found your father's body floating in the shallows where the Saluda River feeds into the lake. You wouldn't happen to know anything about that, would you?"

In as calm of a voice as possible, Connor Knoxx looked Detective Amy Stone directly in the face, shook his head, and said, "No, I have no idea what happened to him. The last time I saw him, he was tearing out of here on that jet ski like a coward."

"So, you have absolutely no idea how your father ended up dead in the river?" Cross asked.

"Nope. I don't have a clue," Connor replied as he held Cross' gaze, "Do you know what happened?"

Stone replied, "He had a nasty gash on his forehead, so it appears to have been some accident while trying to evade law enforcement. The coroner found no signs of foul play, and since he had been in the water for a while, there were no other fingerprints or DNA."

"Well, we just wanted to come and tell you personally," Cross replied.

"Thank you for coming out. That's a shame about my father, though," Connor replied stoically.

Stone and Cross shook hands with Connor Knoxx, and before they left, Stone said, "If you ever need to talk."

"I know where to find you, but like I said, my therapy is out there," Connor replied as he glanced toward the lake.

With that, Stone and Cross turned and walked back to their car, and as Stone turned the car around and started driving off, Cross asked, "You don't believe that crap, do you?"

Stone replied, "Nope, but that's a crime for another day. What do you say we grab a beer tonight after work?"

"Sounds good to me," Cross replied with a smile.

"I'm going to invite my ex-partner too if that's ok. I need to do a little fence mending."

"The more the merrier," Cross replied.

LATER THAT NIGHT, Stone's ex-partner, Drew Clayton, and his girlfriend, Courtney King, walked into the local bar to find Cross and Stone seated in a booth off to the side. They walked over, and Clayton said somberly, "Since you've invited me for drinks, I'll assume you know that I had nothing to do with anything."

"Have a seat," Stone said dryly.

Clayton slid into the booth directly across from Stone, and Courtney King slid in at the end, facing Cross. A waitress took their drink order when the two newcomers slid into the booth. Stone sat silently until the waitress left, and then she finally said, "Clayton, look, I'm sorry. You know how it is. We were following the facts as we knew them."

"It's true," Cross said as Clayton looked to him for validation.

"So, what happened?" Clayton asked.

Stone took a deep breath and replied, "We're still not exactly sure what started all of this, but we know more than we did. Apparently, Dexter Knoxx was very good at the import and export business, and one of his main clients was none other than the Harringtons. Beatrice's husband, who had been buying, selling, and stealing precious art for years, used Dexter Knoxx's network to move his artwork. That's why neither one was ever caught. Anyway, when the whole debacle with the Harrington estate went down, that put a spotlight on the lake and the entire network."

"Okay, I'm with you so far," Clayton replied. What does that have to do with what happened recently?"

Cross replied, "In the information we found in Watts' place, we found blackmail records going back years. Once the spotlight was on the lake, Knoxx retired for good. The only problem was that there were too many people who knew things about him and his operation. Knoxx knew Watts was a veteran with ... issues and started pushing his buttons."

Stone said, "Yeah, and it didn't take long before Watts started eliminating the people that Dexter Knoxx told him to take care of. Watts knew of the lake's history and the old Indian witch stories since he grew up here and used it to his advantage. The only thing Dexter didn't realize was how unstable Watts really was."

"Wait a minute then," Clayton said. "So, how did your father's murder fit into all of this?"

Stone sighed and replied, "Apparently, he knew something was still happening around the lake, but he didn't realize that O'Neil was also working for Dexter Knoxx. I have no evidence, but I suspect that O'Neil did, in fact, try to recruit you years ago in an attempt to put more pressure on my father, but it didn't work, so Dexter had O'Neil kill my father because he was getting too close, which brings us back to why Watts killed O'Neil."

"Well, what about the first victim then? Why was he killed?" Clayton asked.

Stone replied, "Apparently, Jeramy Donahue discovered something he shouldn't have and was trying to bleed Dexter Knoxx dry. We don't know what that is, but he was getting regular payments from Dexter Knoxx, and as far as we can tell, Dexter got tired of paying."

"Well, if all that's what happened ... what happened to Dexter Knoxx?" Clayton asked.

Cross looked at Stone, who paused a moment and said, "I think the Saluda Indian witch just took its last victim."

TETELESTAI